Rachel Renée Russell

with Nikki Russell and Erin Russell

SIMON & SCHUSTER

First published in Great Britain in 2009 by Simon & Schuster UK Ltd

This edition published 2023

First published in the USA in 2009 as *Dork Diaries: Tales from a Not-So-Fabulous Life*,
by Aladdin, an imprint of Simon & Schuster Children's Publishing Division,
1230 Avenue of the Americas, New York, New York 10020

1 3 5 7 9 10 8 6 4 2

Simon & Schuster UK Ltd
1st Floor, 222 Gray's Inn Road
London WC1X 8HB

www.simonandschuster.co.uk
www.simonandschuster.com.au
www.simonandschuster.co.in

Simon & Schuster Australia, Sydney
Simon & Schuster India, New Delhi

A CIP catalogue record for this book is available from the British Library.

PB ISBN 978-1-3985-2755-3
eBook ISBN 978-0-85707-674-8

Printed and Bound in the UK using 100% Renewable
Electricity at CPI Group (UK) Ltd

To my daughter, Nikki,
who tried her hardest to be the best
little ant in the ant colony, when all along
she was a beautiful butterfly

SATURDAY, AUGUST 31

Sometimes I wonder if my life is just a REALLY BAD DREAM. Then there are days when I know it is.

Like today.

The drama started this morning when I casually asked if she would buy me one of those cool new cell phones that do almost everything. I considered it a necessity of life, second only to maybe oxygen.

What better way to clinch a spot in the CCP (Cute, Cool & Popular) group at my new private school, Westchester Country Day, than by dazzling them with a wicked new cell.

Last year, it seemed like I was the ONLY student in my ENTIRE middle school who didn't have one ☹. So I bought an older, used phone SUPERcheap on eBay.

It was bigger than what I wanted, but I figured I couldn't go wrong for the clearance price of only $12.99.

I put my telephone in my locker and spread the word that I had HOT gossip about my NEW phone and that everyone could now call me.

Then I counted down the minutes before my social life started heating up.

I got really nervous when two of the CCP girls came walking down the hall in my direction, chatting on their cell phones. . . .

ME

They came right over to my locker and started acting SUPERfriendly.

Then they invited me to sit with them at lunch and I was like, "Umm . . . okay." But deep down inside I was jumping up and down and doing my Snoopy "happy dance." . . .

Then things got really strange.

They said they had heard the hot gossip about my brand-new iPhone and that everyone (meaning the rest of the CCP crew) was DYING to see it.

I was about to explain that I'd said "I had HOT gossip about my NEW phone" NOT "the HOT gossip is about my NEW iPhone," but I never got a chance because, unfortunately, my telephone started ringing.

Very loudly.

I was trying my best to ignore it, but both of the CCP girls were staring at me like, "Well, aren't you going to answer it?!" . . .

Obviously, I didn't want to answer it because I had a really bad feeling they were going to be a little disappointed when they actually saw my phone.

So I just stood there praying that it would stop ringing, but it didn't.

And pretty soon, everyone in the hallway was staring at me too.

Finally, I gave in, snatched open my locker, and answered the phone. Mainly to stop that AWFUL ringing. . . .

I was like, "Umm . . . sorry. Wrong number."

And when I turned around, both of the CCP girls were running down the hall screaming, "Make it go away! Make it go away!" I guessed it probably meant they DIDN'T want me to sit with them at lunch anymore, which was really HUMILIATING!

The most important lesson I learned last year was

that having a CRUDDY phone—or NONE at all—can totally RUIN your social life. While millions of kids regularly FORGET their homework, not a single one would be caught DEAD without their cell phone. Which was why I was nagging my mom about getting ME one.

I've tried saving up my own money to buy it, but that was impossible to do. Mainly because I'm an artist and TOTALLY ADDICTED to drawing! Like, if I don't do it every day, I'll go NUTZ!

I spend ALL of my cash on sketchbooks, pencils, pens, art camp, and other stuff.

Hey, I'm so BROKE, I have a milk shake on credit at McDonald's!

Anyway, when Mom came home from the mall with a special back-to-school present for me, I was pretty sure I knew what it was.

She rambled on and on about how my attending a new private school was going to be a "stressful time of tremendous personal growth" and how my best "coping mechanism" would be to "communicate" my "thoughts and feelings."

I was absolutely

ECSTATIC

because you can communicate with a

NEW CELL PHONE!

Right?! ☺

I kind of zoned out on most of what my mom was saying because I was DAYDREAMING about all of the cool apps, games, and music I was going to download.

It was going to be LOVE AT FIRST SIGHT! . . .

ME AND MY NEW CELL PHONE!!

But after my mom FINALLY finished her little speech, she smiled really big, hugged me, and handed me a BOOK. . . .

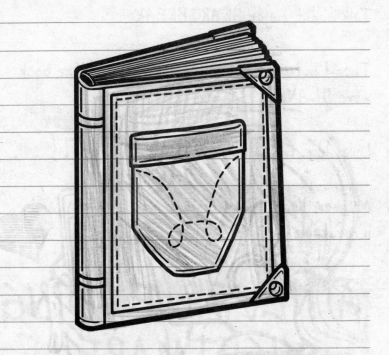

I opened it and FRANTICALLY flipped through the pages, figuring that maybe she had hidden my new cell phone inside.

It made perfect sense at the time because all the advertisements said it was THE thinnest model on the market.

But slowly it dawned on me that my mom had NOT gotten me a cell phone, and my so-called present was just a stupid little book! ☹

Talk about major HEARTBREAK!

Then I noticed that ALL the pages of the book were BLANK.

I was like, OH. NO. SHE. DIDN'T!

My mom had given me two things: a DIARY and irrefutable evidence my life IS, in fact,

A NEVER-ENDING NIGHTMARE!!

Absolutely no one writes their most intimate feelings and deep, dark secrets in a diary anymore! WHY?!

Because just one or two people knowing all your BIZ could completely RUIN your reputation.

You're supposed to post this kind of juicy stuff online on your BLOG so MILLIONS can read it!!! . . .

Only a TOTAL DORK would be caught WRITING in a DIARY!! This is THE worst present I have ever received in my entire life!

I wanted to yell at the top of my lungs: "Mom, I don't need a STUPID book with 336 BLANK pages!!"

What I NEED is to be able to "communicate" my "thoughts and feelings" to my friends using my very own cell phone.

Wait! Silly me. I keep forgetting. I don't have any friends. YET. But that could change overnight, and I need to be prepared. With a shiny new cell!

In the meantime, I will NOT write in this diary again.

NEVER! EVER!!

Okay. I know I said I'd never write in this diary again. I meant it at the time.

I'm definitely not the kind of girl who curls up with a diary and a box of Godiva chocolates to write a bunch of really sappy stuff about

MY DREAMY BOYFRIEND,

MY FIRST KISS,

or my overwhelming ANGST about the HORRIFIC discovery that I'm a

PRINCESS

of a small French-speaking principality and now worth

BILLIONS!!

THIS IS SO <u>NOT</u> ME!

Pedicure

Cute, flirty habit of
twirling hair that drives
the guys wild!

Beauty   Manicure

Brains   Shiny
Designer   Hair
Clothing

Perfect
Body

Chocolates
(from adoring
boyfriend)

Perfect Skin

Exciting
Diary

Princess
Tiara

MY LIFE TOTALLY SUCKS!! All day I wandered around my new school like a ZOMBIE in lip gloss. Not a single person bothered to say hi.

THIS IS ME!

MOST OF THE TIME
I FEEL INVISIBLE!

How am I supposed to fit in at a snobby prep school like Westchester Country Day?! This place has a Starbucks in the cafeteria!

I wish my dad had NEVER been awarded a bug extermination contract from this school.

They can take their little pity scholarship and give it to someone who wants and needs it, because I sure DON'T!

It's way past midnight, and I'm about to freak out because I still don't have my homework done.

I was really surprised to hear a knock on my bedroom door this late at night, and I assumed it was my six-year-old sister, Brianna.

About a week ago, she lost one of her front teeth and buried it in the backyard to see if it would grow.

She is FOREVER doing weird stuff like that.

My mom says it's because she's still a little kid. But I personally think it's because she has the IQ of a box of crayons.

As a little joke, I told Brianna the tooth fairy collected teeth from children all over the world and then superglued them together to make dentures for old people.

I explained that she was in BIG TROUBLE with the tooth fairy, seeing as she had dug a hole and buried her tooth somewhere out in the backyard.

The funniest part was that Brianna TOTALLY believed me.

She actually dug up half of Mom's flower garden trying to find her tooth.

Since then Brianna has been paranoid that the tooth fairy is going to sneak into her room in the middle of the night and pull out ALL her teeth to make dentures.

But my prank kind of backfired, because now she absolutely REFUSES to use the bathroom at night unless I first check inside to make sure the tooth fairy is not hiding behind the shower curtain or under the bath towels.

And if I'm not quick enough, Brianna will have a little "accident" right on my bedroom carpet.

MY LITTLE SISTER, BRIANNA

Unfortunately, I had to learn the hard way that (contrary to the TV commercial) Carpet Fresh DOES NOT remove all odors.

But it wasn't Brianna at my door—it was my parents. . . .

MOM

DAD

Before I could say "Come in," they just kind of barged in like they always do, which really irritated me because this is SUPPOSED to be MY room!

And I have a constitutional right to PRIVACY, which they keep invading.

The next time my parents and Brianna come rollin' up in here, I'm gonna scream . . .

"HEY! WHY DON'T YOU PEOPLE JUST MOVE IN?!"

Anyway, my parents said they were surprised to see that I was still up doing homework, and they wanted to know how things were going at school.

It was really strange, because just as I was about to answer, I had a total meltdown right on the spot and burst into tears. . . .

My parents were shocked and stared at me and then at each other.

Finally, Mom hugged me and said, "My poor little Boo-Boo!" which only made me feel WORSE.

Not fitting in at school was bad enough. But now I had to suffer the additional humiliation of being the only fourteen-year-old STILL being called "little Boo-Boo"! Suddenly my dad's face lit up.

"Hey, I've got a great idea! We know you've been under a lot of stress lately with our move and your new school. I bet if we posted some positive affirmations all around the house, it would help you adjust. What do you think?"

I was like, "Okay, Dad, THIS is what I think: It's a STUPID idea! Like sticky notes with corny sayings on them will solve my problem of being a TOTAL LOSER at school. You wanna know what else I think? The article I read about bug extermination chemicals killing off brain cells is probably true!"

But I just said it inside my head, so no one else heard it but me.

My parents kept staring at me, and it was starting to creep me out.

Finally, after what seemed like forever, my mom smiled and said, "Honey, just remember, we love you! And if you need us, we're right down the hall."

They walked back to their bedroom, and for several minutes, I could hear their muffled voices. I guessed that they were probably discussing whether or not to deal with my raging hormones right then or first thing in the morning.

Since it was so late, I decided to finish my homework during study hall.

It feels like I'm dealing with a case of Toxic Teen Turmoil.

What if it's contagious?!

Maybe I should just stay home from school tomorrow and sleep in :-)!

My new issue of *That's So Hot!* magazine says the secret to happiness is the four *Fs*:

Friends, Fun, Fashion & Flirting

But, unfortunately, the closest I've ever gotten to "friends, fun, fashion, and flirting" is having a locker right next to MacKenzie Hollister.

She's THE most popular girl in the eighth grade.

Lucky me! ☹

I had just finished fighting my way through the crowded hallways to get to my locker and had almost been trampled alive.

Then, suddenly, as if by magic, the huge mob of students parted right down the center, just like the Red Sea. That's when I first saw MacKenzie strutting down the hallway like it was the runway of a Paris fashion show or something.

She had blond hair and blue eyes and was dressed like she had just finished a photo shoot for the cover of *Teen Vogue*.

And everyone (except me) immediately fell under her powerful hypnotic spell and totally lost their minds.

"What's up, MacKenzie!"

"You look fabulous, MacKenzie!"

"Are you coming to my party this weekend, MacKenzie?"

"Your shoes are to die for, MacKenzie!"

"Will you marry me, MacKenzie?"

"You'll NEVER guess who has a crush on you, MacKenzie!"

"Is that ANOTHER designer purse, MacKenzie?"

"Love your hair today, MacKenzie!"

"I'll pluck out my eye with a pencil and eat it with a Spam and mustard sandwich IF ONLY you'll sit with me at lunch today, MacKenzie!"

Which also proves my theory that there's ALWAYS at least ONE WEIRDO in EVERY middle school around the WORLD!

It was "MacKenzie! MacKenzie! MacKenzie!" When she walked up to the locker right next to mine, I knew then and there I was going to have a VERY bad school year.

Being so close to the radiance of her awesome
yet sickening perfection just made me feel like a
humongous LOSER. And it didn't help that she was
HOGGING most of my personal space ☺!!

Hey, it wasn't like I was jealous of her or anything. I mean, how totally juvenile would THAT be?!

Between classes, MacKenzie and her friends are FOREVER standing right in front of MY locker, "GGG-ing." That means:
GIGGLING, GOSSIPING, AND GLOSSING!

And whenever I get up the nerve to say, "Excuse me, but I really need to get into my locker," she just ignores me or rolls her eyes and says stuff like "Annoying much?" or "What's HER problem?"

And I'm like, "Hey, girlfriend! I don't have no STINKIN' problem!"

But I just say it inside my head, so no one really hears it except me.

However, deep down I'm troubled and ashamed that a tiny part of me—a very dark and primitive side—would totally LOVE to be best friends with MacKenzie! . . .

MACKENZIE AND ME AS BFFS!

And I find that part of myself SO DISGUSTING . . .
I could . . . VOMIT!

But on a much happier note, I'm really into lip gloss
too. My favorite one right now is Krazy Kissalicious
Strawberry Crush Glitterati. It's yummy and tastes
just like strawberry cheesecake.

Unfortunately, no supercute hunk (like Brandon Roberts, the guy who sits in front of me in my biology class) has developed a huge crush on me and fallen in love with my fabulous glossy lips, like in all of those KRAZY KISSALICIOUS television commercials.

But hey! It could happen!

Oh, I almost forgot! Dad is supposed to pick me up after school today to take me to my dentist appointment.

PLEASE, PLEASE, PLEASE don't let him pick me up in his work van with the five-foot-long plastic roach on top.

I would absolutely DIE if anyone saw his van and found out I only attend this school due to his bug extermination contract!

MacKenzie and her snobby friends are always making NASTY comments about any girl who wanders within six feet of them. I mean, who do they think they are?

HI, HON! YOU'RE UNDER ARREST FOR A FELONY FASHION VIOLATION!

THE FASHION POLICE?!

Well, today I was the FASHION FELON!

I was at my locker getting my books when, in under one minute, MacKenzie gave ME the following scathing fashion commentary while applying her lip gloss:

"OMG! I bought that exact same sweater Nikki is wearing! For my DOG, from Pets-N-Stuff."

"Don't you need a LICENSE to be that UGLY?"

"That outfit would be perfect for Goodwill. If she knows what's GOOD for her, she WILL burn it."

"What's that awful STANK?! She's supposed to spray on the perfume, not marinate in it."

"She has SO much acne, she uses a special makeup brand. It's called Why Bother?"

"What's up with her hairstyle? It looks like a small mammal made a nest in her hair, had babies, and died!"

"Nikki thinks she's SO cute. She's just living proof that manure can actually grow legs and walk."

"And what's up with that totally tacky denim DIARY? She's SUCH a DORK!"

OMG! By the time I left my locker, I thought I was going to have a complete meltdown.

I went straight to the girls' bathroom, rushed into a stall, and slammed the door.

Then I flushed the toilet a few times so no one could hear me CRYING!

To call MacKenzie a "mean girl" would be an understatement. She's VICIOUS . . . and CRUEL! She's a PIT BULL in glittery eye shadow and hair extensions!

Thanks to her, I'll probably be in therapy for the rest of my life!

!

I think I've finally figured out why I don't fit in at this school. According to MacKenzie, I need a new designer wardrobe from one of those really expensive teen shops at the mall.

You know, the ones where the salesgirls dress like models and have blond highlights, perfect teeth, and phony smiles.

But what really makes me ANGRY is their nasty habit of unexpectedly snatching open the curtain of your dressing room and popping their head inside when you're changing your clothes.

It's enough to make you want to slap those blond highlights right out of their hair.

And when you look in the mirror, you can obviously see that the outfit looks HORRIBLE on you.

But those salesgirls just smile and act cute and perky and LIE TO YOUR FACE by saying the outfit (1) looks totally fabulous, (2) brings out your natural skin tones, and (3) complements your eye color.

And they'll tell you this EVEN if you're trying on one of those huge green lawn-size TRASH BAGS! . . .

ME, WEARING A PLASTIC TRASH BAG!

I also HATE clothes that are "SNOBBY CHIC." It's when the exact same outfit looks TOTALLY different on two very similar girls. The more popular you are at school, the BETTER it looks on you, and the more unpopular you are, the WORSE it looks on you.

I can't tell you HOW a snobby chic outfit mysteriously knows all of this personal stuff about you, but it obviously DOES!

WHY I HATE SNOBBY CHIC FASHIONS!

The SNOBBY CHIC phenomenon is quite a mind-boggling thing.

Hopefully, Congress will allocate funding for scientists to study it, along with how socks mysteriously disappear from the dryer.

But, until then,

BUYER BEWARE ☹!

SATURDAY, SEPTEMBER 7

I'm really SICK and TIRED of MacKenzie's MEAN GIRL attitude and antics.

So I've decided I'm going to walk right up to that spoiled-rotten DIVA and tell her off really good.

My magazine says every girl needs to be friendly and find her own inner beauty deep down inside.

But I say every girl needs to be smart and strong and IGNORE all the HATERS!

I'm going to tell MacKenzie right to her face (on like maybe the last day of school) that just because she and her friends dress like FASHIONISTAS, they do NOT have the right to say nasty things about other people.

"People" being the girls whose moms make them shop at JCPenney, Sears, and other stores like that.

Girls like . . . well, ME!

40

Okay. It's NOT a big secret that the clothes from those stores AREN'T as COOL as the clothes from the mall.

And yes, it's a huge inconvenience (and a definite turnoff) to have to walk through the "Old Ladies Dept," "Mom's Dept," and "Pregnant Ladies Dept" to get to the one for "TEENS." . . .

FINDING THE TEEN DEPARTMENT

No wonder most girls prefer those fancy teen shops in the mall!

My mom says it really doesn't matter where your clothes come from as long as they're clean.

Right?

WRONG!!

I don't know how many times I've heard MacKenzie shriek, "OMG! WHERE are these PATHETIC girls buying such HIDEOUS clothes?! The Dollar Store? Sorry, but I'd come to school butt naked before I would EVER buy my fashions from a store that sells LAWN MOWERS!"

To be honest, I didn't know the stores I shopped at sold lawn mowers. And even if they do, big fat hairy deal! It's not like the clothes smell like a lawn mower or something. At least, I hadn't noticed it. The next time I go shopping, I'm going to sniff the clothing before I buy anything, just to make sure.

I'm also going to wear a hat, wig, sunglasses, and phony mustache so no one will recognize me. . . .

WHATEVER!!

I'm already dreading that I have to go back to school tomorrow. It's been one whole week, and I still haven't made a single friend. I've got this . . . OVERWHELMING . . . sense of LONELINESS . . . sitting in the pit of my stomach like a . . .

BIG FAT POISONOUS . . . TOAD!

I'm seriously thinking about asking my parents to let me move back to the city and live with my grandma so I can attend my old school.

I'll admit the school wasn't perfect. But I'd give anything to hang out with my friends from art class again. I really, really miss them ☹!

Anyway, my grandma lives in one of those apartment buildings for elderly people "who are young at heart and committed to leading a full and active life." So she's up on ALL the latest fads and stuff. She's also a little wacky (okay, A LOT WACKY) and totally addicted to the game show *The Price Is Right*.

Last year Grandma bought a computer from the Home Shopping Network to help her train to be a contestant on *The Price Is Right*.

Now she spends most of her spare time on her computer, memorizing the suggested retail prices of all the major grocery store brands.

She plans to use all her research and game strategies

to write a how-to manual called *The Price Is Right for Really Stupid People.*

Grandma says her book could be bigger than Harry Potter. . . .

MY GRANDMA

I didn't think being on a game show took any special skills, but she told me you had to train like you would for the Super Bowl.

She took a few sips of her energy drink, stared at me real seriouslike, and whispered, "Sweetie, when life presents challenges, you can be either a CHICKEN or a CHAMPION. The choice is YOURS!"

Then she started humming the song "Girls Just Want to Have Fun" really loud.

I was like, JUST GREAT! Grandma is finally going SENILE!

Doesn't she understand that some things in life you're STUCK with and powerless to change?! Give me a break!

But I have to admit, she has gotten pretty good at *The Price Is Right.*

The last few times I saw her play along with the game show, she got every single price correct!

It was amazing because she would have won like $549,321 in cash and prizes, including three cars, a boat, a trip for two to Niagara Falls, and a lifetime supply of Depends adult diapers.

I gave her a big hug and said, "Grandma, you have mad skillz at the *Price Is Right* game, and I'm really proud of you. But you should really try to get out of the house more often."

Grandma just smiled and said her life is exciting now that she's taking hip-hop dance lessons at the senior rec center. And her dance teacher, Krump Daddy, is "dope!" Then she asked me if I wanted to see her "bust a move."

I was like, "Thanks, Grandma. But I probably should get started on my homework right now."

I was actually really worried she was going to BUST her hip, skull, or spleen and I'd have to call 911.

Then my parents would blame ME because my grandma almost KILLED herself doing hip-hop.

49

But she disappeared for a few minutes and came back into the room wearing a hot-pink warm-up suit and carrying a huge old-school boom box. Then . . .

MY GRANDMA, SLAYING THOSE
DANCE MOVES!!

I was SUPERimpressed.

She was actually really good for a seventy-six-
year-old!

And her tunes were **superCOOL**, too.

Grandma's a little **WACKY**, but you gotta
LOVE her!

☺!!

This morning the halls were plastered with colorful posters for Random Acts of Avant-Garde Art, our annual school art show.

I'm SUPERexcited because the first prize for each class is $750, cash! SWEET! That would be enough for me to get a cell phone, a new outfit from the mall, AND art supplies.

But most important, winning that award could transform me from a "socially challenged ART DORK" to a "socially charmed ART DIVA" practically overnight!

Then maybe someone at this school would want to be my friend.

So I rushed down to the school office to get an entry form and was surprised to see a line had already formed.

And guess who else was there picking one up too?

MACKENZIE ☹!!!!

And as usual she was blabbering nonstop: "Like, since I'm going to be a model/fashion designer/pop star, I've created some HOT fashion illustrations for my FAB-4-EVER clothing line, which I also plan to wear on my successful world tour so all of my ADORING fans will see MY designs and buy like a million dollars' worth. Then I'm going to enroll at a prestigious university like Harvard, Yale, or the Westchester Fashion Institute of Cosmetology, which, BTW, is owned by my aunt Clarissa!"

Okay. I'll admit I FREAKED OUT about having to compete against MacKenzie.

She just kept staring at me with her icy blue eyes, and my stomach felt queasy and I got chill bumps. Then, suddenly, I had an epiphany and I TOTALLY understood what my grandma meant when she said,

"You can be either a CHICKEN or a CHAMPION. The choice is yours."

53

I took a deep breath as my heart pounded in my chest. The choice I was about to make could impact the rest of my life.

It took a lot of courage to admit I was . . .

ME

A BIG FAT CHICKEN!

When the office assistant asked if I was there to pick up an entry form for the avant-garde art show, I just froze and started clucking like a hen:

BUK, BUK, BUK-KA-A-AH!

Then MacKenzie laughed, like ME entering the competition was the most RIDICULOUS thing she had ever heard.

That's when I spotted the yellow sign-up sheet for library shelving assistants, also known as LSAs.

Every day during study hall, a few kids get excused to go to the school library to shelve books.

An LSA's life is about as exciting as watching paint dry.

So, instead of trying to achieve my dream of winning a major art competition, I very STUPIDLY signed up to shelve DUSTY and BORING LIBRARY BOOKS! . . .

MY FUTURE MISERABLE LIFE AS A
LIBRARY SHELVING ASSISTANT

And it's ALL MacKenzie's fault!! ☹

When I reported to the library during study hall, the librarian, Mrs. Peach, gave me a tour. She told me I would be working with two other girls who had signed up last week.

But what I wanted to know was WHO in their right mind would sign up to shelve library books as an EXTRACURRICULAR ACTIVITY?!

How about three desperate, socially challenged DORKS!!

I CAN'T believe MacKenzie has TOTALLY WRECKED my life like this!!

I had the most horrible accident in French class today.

While I was taking my French book out of my backpack, my perfumed body spray, called Sassy Sasha, fell on the floor.

Unfortunately, the little white nozzle thingy popped off, and it just kept spraying and spraying until the entire can was empty.

My teacher, Mr. Somethin' or Other (I can't pronounce his name because it sounds like a sneeze), started yelling a lot of stuff in French that sounded an awful lot like curse words.

Then he evacuated all the students from the classroom because everyone was coughing and choking and their eyes were watering really bad.

And while we were standing in the hallway, waiting

for the smell to go away, he asked me very rudely in English (which I DO understand) if I was trying to KILL him.

Okay! First of all, I don't like French class that much anyway.

And second of all, it was JUST an accident!

I mean, it's NOT like my perfume was REALLY going to kill him.

At least, I don't think so.

But, then again, WHAT if it actually DID?!

What if my French teacher collapsed in the teachers' lounge while eating a corn dog at lunch and died from extreme Sassy Sasha asphyxiation??!!

And what if, for three whole days, no one noticed the foul odor coming from his dead body, since the school lunches normally smell a lot like rotting flesh too?! . . .

STINK FUMES

MY FRENCH TEACHER

The police would launch an investigation, and I would be the main suspect.

Then the crime-scene experts would conduct scientific tests on my French teacher's nose hairs and find traces of Sassy Sasha.

They would figure out that he was fumigated with a lethal dose of perfume body spray.

And what if someone who HATED my GUTS (like, um, MacKenzie Hollister!) SECRETLY planted incriminating physical evidence to make it look like I committed a vicious, premeditated MURDER! . . .

A MURDER INVESTIGATION

POLICE

YOU GOTTA BELIEVE ME. I'M TOTALLY INNOCENT!

I'd end up getting a LIFE SENTENCE during my
freshman year, which would NOT be very FUN!
And then afterward, I'd be highly upset because I
also MISSED OUT on drivers' ed class, my senior
prom, high school graduation, college, my wedding,
my children's births, becoming a grandmother, and
DYING at eighty-nine in a cold, lonely nursing home!

Now that I think about it, my French teacher just
LOVES MacKenzie, because she's really good at
French and she can pronounce his weird sneeze-
sounding name.

I bet if she had dropped HER Sassy Sasha body
spray in his classroom and the nozzle thingy popped
off, he would NOT have yelled at her or accused
her of trying to kill him. But that's because
MacKenzie is

MISS PERFECT!!

I bet she's even going to WIN the avant-garde art
competition!

And afterward, just out of spite, she'll probably check out, like, 389 books from the school library and then return them all the next day.

Of course, I'LL be the one STUCK having to put each and every one of them away, since I'm a STUPID library shelving assistant!

My pathetic life is SO UNFAIR, it makes me want to

SCREAM!

☹!!

Today everyone in the cafeteria was SUPERexcited because MacKenzie was handing out invitations to her big birthday bash. . . .

MACKENZIE, HANDING OUT
PARTY INVITATIONS!

Guys were high-fiving one another, and girls, like Lisa Wang and Sarah Cohen, were crying and hugging one another like they had just scored tickets to a sold-out concert of their favorite boy band.

It was beyond DISGUSTING!

For the rest of the day, everyone MacKenzie invited to her party sucked up to her like human vacuum cleaners. Except for BRANDON ROBERTS.

When she gave him an invitation, she tried to flirt with him by twirling her hair around her finger and smiling really big. She even "accidentally" dropped her purse on purpose so he would pick it up for her.

But Brandon just glanced at MacKenzie's invitation, shoved it into his backpack, and walked right past her.

And, boy, did she get upset when he blew her off like that.

Then a bunch of jocks trampled all over her expensive new designer purse before she could pick it up off the floor. Personally, I kind of liked the dirty footprints better than that boring floral pattern.

Anyway, Brandon is SOOOO COOOOL!!!

From what I can tell, he seems to be kind of the quiet rebel type.

He's a reporter and photographer for the school newspaper and has won a few awards for his photojournalism.

Once he actually sat at my lunch table, but I don't think he noticed me staring at him. Probably because his shaggy, wavy hair is FOREVER falling into his eyes.

And today in biology, when he asked if he could take a picture for the school newspaper of ME dissecting my frog, I almost FAINTED!!

I was shaking so badly, I could hardly hold the scalpel. But now every tiny detail of his perfect face is permanently etched in my mind.

IS IT POSSIBLE THAT I AM *FALLING IN LOVE* FOR THE FIRST TIME?!

SQUEEE!

THE BIOLOGY OF MY HEARTBREAK
By Nikki Maxwell

I see you in my dreams
in your favorite white
button-down shirt,
sitting across from me
in the cafeteria.
I've never seen anyone
eat fries so beautifully.

I see you in biology class,
taking pictures for
the school newspaper, when
you whisper to the depths of my soul,
"Hold the frog at an angle."

For it is only you
who can make a photo
of a dissected frog
seem so vibrant.
So alive. Yet dead.

It hurts to feel this way,
to know that you'll never know me.
To want to run my fingers
through your dark, wavy hair,
as I realize that
the putrid smell of formaldehyde
and the dull gaze of a lifeless frog
will forever remind ME of US!

I'M TOTALLY CRUSHING ON BRANDON!

During my PE class, even the Scared-of-Balls girls were gossiping about MacKenzie's party.

But I'm pretty sure they didn't get invited either.

They're the really prissy girls who hang in small groups and scream hysterically whenever a ball comes near them.

It could be a:

basketball, football, baseball, soccer ball, tennis ball, volleyball, beach ball, Ping-Pong ball, mothball, or even . . .

a meatball.

They're NOT very picky.

SCARED-OF-BALLS GIRLS PLAY VOLLEYBALL

Red team WINS by 1 point! Your grade is A⁺. LOSERS, hit the showers! Your grade is C.

PE TEACHER

YEP! You can always count on the Scared-of-Balls girls to mess things up and lose the game for you.

It's really cruddy to have girls like Chloe and Zoey on your team. Especially if you absolutely HATE taking showers after PE class (just the thought of showering at school makes me nauseous).

It will totally be THEIR fault if I catch some kind of incurable disease from the slimy mold and mildew growing in those NASTY showers.

WHY I HATE SHOWERING IN PE CLASS!

I was really surprised when Chloe and Zoey came up to me after PE class and started talking. Of course, I pretended like I was NOT SUPERangry at them for running away from the ball and making me FILTHY from taking that nasty shower.

Apparently, Mrs. Peach told them I was assigned to work with them in the library, and they were actually EXCITED about it.

Like, **WHAT** is so exciting about shelving library books??!!

But I just played along and pretended to be as thrilled about it as they were.

I was like, "OMG! OMG! I can't believe we're going to be shelving books together. How COOL is that?!"

We ended up eating lunch together at table 9, and it was really nice NOT having to eat alone for once.

Chloe's full name is Chloe Christina Garcia, and she is Latina. Her family owns a software company.

It was amazing because she has read, like, ALL of the latest novels.

She says she lives "vicariously" through the characters' joys and heartbreaks and learns a lot of stuff about life, love, boys, and kissing, which she plans to use when she goes to high school next year.

She said she owns 983 books and has read most of them twice.

I was like, "WOW!"

Zoey's full name is Zoeysha Ebony Franklin, and she is African-American. Her mom is an attorney and her dad is a record company executive.

She has met practically ALL of the biggest pop stars and says they're just normal people.

Zoey says she likes reading self-help and inspirational books because they help her to appreciate the simple joys of living.

She explained, "Now I have a mom AND a stepmother. Having just ONE overbearing mother figure in your life can sometimes be challenging and mentally exhausting. But can you imagine having TWO?! OMG!"

Then Zoey said, "Nikki, how can you stand having a locker next to MacKenzie's? She's so SHALLOW, she rubs lipstick on her forehead to make up her mind! And being SUPERconceited can sometimes develop into a narcissistic personality disorder."

I could NOT believe Zoey actually said that.

I thought EVERYONE at this school worshipped MacKenzie.

We laughed so hard that chewed-up carrot bits shot right out of my nose! . . .

CHLOE, ZOEY, AND ME, LAUGHING
OUR BUTTS OFF!

All three of us were like, "EWW! GROSS!"

Then Chloe said, "Hey! Carrot-flavored boogers!
Let's give them to MacKenzie so she can
sprinkle them over her tofu salad as a low-carb
topping!"

We laughed so hard at Chloe's joke that the kids sitting at tables 6 and 8 started staring at us.

I even saw MacKenzie glance our way. But then she looked away really fast so we wouldn't make the huge mistake of thinking she actually acknowledged our existence. I could tell she was wondering what was going on.

Anyway, I had a BLAST with Chloe and Zoey at lunch today. So I've forgiven them for that shower FIASCO in PE class.

I can't wait to hang out with them every day in the library. Who would have THUNK I'd actually look forward to being an LSA and shelving books?

I could TOTALLY be BFFs with Chloe and Zoey! Because all three of us are a little

KA-RAY-ZEE!

☺!!

I was pretty SICK and TIRED of hearing about MacKenzie and her STUPID little party! But since she is in my geometry class and I sit right behind her, I knew I was just going to have to deal with it. I was trying my best to ignore her when she turned around, smiled at me, and did the STRANGEST thing!

MACKENZIE

She handed ME a bright pink invitation tied with a big white satin bow!

I gasped and almost fell out of my chair. My brain was like

OMG! OMG! OMG!

It was the most beautiful thing I had ever seen, other than maybe that new cell phone I want. Who would have thought that I would get an invitation to THE party of the year?! Then it dawned on me that this might be some kind of really cruel JOKE.

So I looked around the room for a hidden camera or something. That's when I realized that most of the other girls in my class were staring at me with envy and disbelief.

It was really weird, because suddenly I noticed I had tiny lint balls all over my favorite hoodie. And it made me feel self-conscious, so I tried to pick a few of them off.

None of MacKenzie's friends would be caught dead in a not-from-the-mall hoodie with lint balls on it.

So I made a mental note . . .

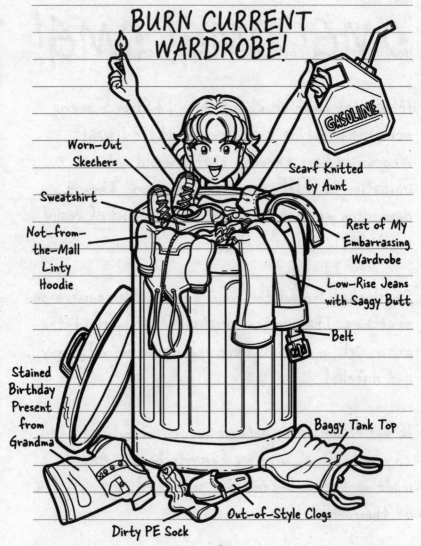

BURN CURRENT WARDROBE!

Worn-Out Skechers

Scarf Knitted by Aunt

Sweatshirt

Not-from-the-Mall Linty Hoodie

Rest of My Embarrassing Wardrobe

Low-Rise Jeans with Saggy Butt

Belt

Stained Birthday Present from Grandma

Baggy Tank Top

Out-of-Style Clogs

Dirty PE Sock

MacKenzie was still smiling at me like I was her new BFF or something.

"Hey, hon! I was just wondering if you would—?"

But I was SO excited, I jumped right in and interrupted her before she could even finish her sentence.

"MacKenzie, I would LOVE to!" I gushed. "Thanks for asking me . . . hon!"

Okay. So I actually called her "hon," even though I always thought that word sounded SUPERphony.

And yes, I was HAPPY and relieved that FINALLY MacKenzie had STOPPED treating me like some kind of diseased, fashion-challenged, um . . . LOSER!

But mostly I was in SHOCK. I could hardly believe I was actually going to MacKenzie's party! Soon I was going to have friends AND a social life.

OMG! WHAT if I ended up with a BOYFRIEND?! I would literally just pee my pants!!

I was starting to believe my *That's So Hot!* magazine was right. Maybe the key to happiness really was friends, fun, fashion, and flirting!!

SQUEEEEEEEE!!!

I felt like I was floating on air, surrounded by sunshine, rainbows, twinkling stars, and pink cotton-candy clouds as I passionately clutched my invitation to MacKenzie's party over my heart!!

My hands were trembling as I untied the ribbon and tore open the envelope.

Suddenly, MacKenzie narrowed her eyes at me and scowled like I was something smeared on the bottom of her shoe.

"You IDIOT!" she hissed. "WHAT are you doing?!"

"Umm, opening m—my invitation?" I stammered.

I was already starting to have a really bad feeling about this whole party thing.

"Like I would invite you?!" She sneered, flipping her blond tresses and batting her long lashes at me in disgust. "Aren't you the new girl who hangs around my locker all the time like some kind of creepy stalker?"

"Well, yes . . . I mean, NO! Actually, my locker is right next to yours," I muttered.

"Are you sure?" she said, looking me up and down like I was lying to her or something. I couldn't believe she was actually pretending like she didn't know me. I've only had a locker next to hers, like, FOREVER!

"I'm VERY sure!" I replied, a little unsure of myself.

Then MacKenzie took out her Krazy Kissalicious lip gloss and applied, like, three extra-thick layers. After gazing at herself in her little compact mirror for an entire minute (she is SO STUCK on herself!), she snapped it shut and glared at me.

"Before you so RUDELY interrupted me, I was simply asking if you would PASS my invitation to JESSICA! How was I supposed to know you were going to rip it open like some uncivilized GORILLA?" Mackenzie spat. . . .

ME?! →

ME, OPENING THE INVITATION

Then everyone in the class turned around and stared at me.

I could NOT believe my ears! How dare that girl actually call me

UNCIVILIZED!!

"Oh. Okay. MY BAD!" I said, trying to sound coolly nonchalant about the whole thing while blinking back tears. "Um, WHO'S Jessica?"

Suddenly I felt a sharp tap on my shoulder.

I turned around to face the girl sitting in the desk behind me.

"I'm Jessica," she announced, rolling her eyes at me. "I can't believe you opened MY invitation!"

I DEFINITELY remembered seeing her hanging out with MacKenzie next to my locker.

She had long blond hair and was wearing glittery pink lip gloss, a pink sweater, a pink miniskirt, and a headband trimmed with fake pink diamonds.

If I had spotted her in Toys "R" Us, I swear I would have probably mistaken her for a new fashion doll:

TOTALLY TICKED-OFF JESSICA....

Totally Ticked-Off Jessica

"Hi, I'm Jessica, and I'm REALLY, REALLY **TICKED!**"

I was desperately trying to tie the satin ribbon back on when Jessica snatched the invitation from my hand so violently, I almost got a paper cut.

I felt like a TOTAL IDIOT! And, to make matters worse, I heard a few of the kids around me snickering.

This was absolutely THE most

EMBARRASSING

moment of my PATHETIC little life!!

And I had no doubt that, in just a matter of minutes, everyone in the ENTIRE school was going to be texting gossip about me.

I was relieved when our geometry teacher, Mrs. Sprague, finally started class.

She spent the entire hour at the board reviewing how to calculate the volume of a cylinder, sphere, and cone for our upcoming test on Monday. . . .

HOW TO CALCULATE VOLUME

The volume of a cylinder equals the (area of the base) × height = $\pi r^2 h$

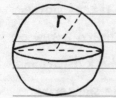

The volume of a sphere = $\frac{4}{3}\pi r^3$

The volume of a cone is $\frac{1}{3}$ the (area of base) x height = $\frac{1}{3} \pi r^2 h$

But I was too freaked out to concentrate on math formulas and was totally NOT listening. I just sat there staring at the back of MacKenzie's head, wishing I could disappear.

I guess I must have been really upset, because a tear rolled down my cheek and splattered my geometry notebook.

But I wiped it up with the sleeve of my not-from-the-mall, lint-ball-covered hoodie before anyone saw it.

Even though I was totally bummed about all the DRAMA over the invitation, I really wasn't that mad at MacKenzie.

I'M SUCH A LOSER!!

If I was having a party, I WOULDN'T invite myself either! . . .

SATURDAY, SEPTEMBER 14

I've had the most HORRIBLE week ever! WHY?
Because MacKenzie has TOTALLY TRASHED my life:

1. She totally RIDICULED me with her cruel fashion
commentary.

2. She RUINED my chances in the avant-garde art
competition.

3. She DISSED me by NOT inviting me to her party.

4. She EMBARRASSED me by calling me an
uncivilized GORILLA.

5. She PUBLICLY HUMILIATED me by giving me an
invitation and then UNINVITING me.

6. She tried to STEAL the one true love of my
life, Brandon Roberts, by inviting him to her party,
flirting with him, and twirling her hair around and
around in a desperate attempt to HYPNOTIZE him
into doing her EVIL bidding.

I planned to spend my ENTIRE weekend just sitting on my bed in my pajamas, STARING at the wall and SULKING. Which, strangely enough, always seems to make me feel a lot better ☺.

ME, SULKING IN MY ROOM

But my plans were completely RUINED!

Around noon my mom came bouncing into my room all cheerful and announced that for lunch we were having a family cookout on the grill.

She said, "Honey, get dressed quick and come out into the backyard and join the FUN!"

Well, obviously, I wasn't in the mood for "fun," and I just wanted to be left alone.

And I don't like hanging out in our backyard, because I have seen some fairly large spiders out there.

I have a "thing" about spiders—they creep me out.

Also, my doctor has diagnosed me as being highly allergic to pests that suck human blood, such as spiders, mosquitoes, ticks, leeches, and vampires.

My life motto is "Bloodsuckers CANNOT be trusted!" . . .

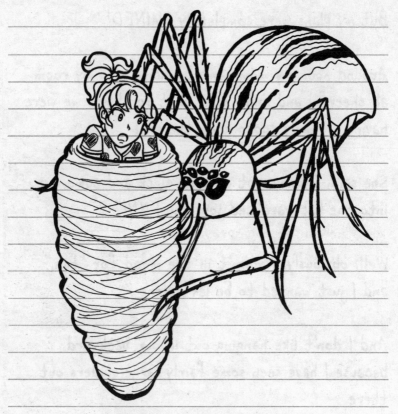

WHY BLOODSUCKERS
CAN'T BE TRUSTED!!

Anyway, when I went outside, my dad was wearing the apron that we got him for Father's Day.

It said "My Dad Is the World's Greatest Cook!" but most of the letters have faded off in the wash, and it now says "My Dad eat s ook!"

He was grilling the meat while whistling old disco tunes. Then, out of the blue, he suddenly developed a major complication. Not with his whistling, but his grilling. I guess you could call it a bug problem. So when he told me to run into the house and get the can of bug spray, I had a really BAD feeling about it.

I was like, "Dad, are you sure?"

And he was like, "I don't plan on sharing my twenty-dollar steaks with these pesky flies."

Well, THAT was a big mistake, because the bugs were NOT pesky flies. You'd think an experienced exterminator would recognize a fly when he saw one. Unfortunately for Dad, he was dealing with a nest of very ANGRY WASPS!! . . .

Kills on Contact!

ZAP

Roach & Ant Killer

NET WT 14 FL OZ

OUR FAMILY BARBECUE PICNIC
(A STORY IN PICTURES)

THE END

Well, our cookout ended up being a total disaster!

To make Dad feel better, we all complimented
him on how handsome he looked in his snazzy
apron, even though he was a little dirty from
knocking over the neighbor lady's garbage cans
when he was running away from those wasps.

POOR DAD ☹!!

However, the good news is that I was able to go
back up to my room and put in a few more hours of
intense sulking. WOO-HOO!

Today we had our math test on calculating volume, and I was SUPERnervous. Mainly because I am not that good at math.

And, just as I had dreaded, my geometry test was REALLY, REALLY hard.

Yes, I know!

I should have studied more. But since I spent the entire weekend

SULKING,

it kind of cut into my study time.

I pretty much just prayed like crazy through the entire test.

Literally!

Sometimes even out loud:

"PLEASE, PLEASE, PLEASE HELP ME TO PASS THIS TEST! I'M REALLY SORRY ABOUT NOT DOING MY CHORES AND TEASING MY LITTLE SISTER, AND I'LL TRY TO DO BETTER. ALSO, CAN YOU TELL ME IF THE FORMULA FOR THE VOLUME OF A CYLINDER IS $\pi r^2 h$ OR $\pi h r^2$? AND, WHEN YOU CALCULATE A SPHERE, DO YOU MULTIPLY THE . . . ?"

I guess a few people sitting near me must have overheard.

I was TOO happy when that test was FINALLY over!

As I was putting my stuff into my backpack to go to my next class, I couldn't help noticing MacKenzie eyeballing me all evil-like.

Then she walked up to Jessica and said, "Today is the last day to enter the avant-garde art competition, and I have to take my entry form down to the office. I'll meet you at my locker, okay?"

Then Jessica stared at me and said really loud, "Mac, I just KNOW you're going to win first place.

Your fashion illustrations are SO, um . . .

FABULICIOUS!"

I could NOT believe Jessica actually said that, because "fabulicious" is, like, so yesterday!

But the thing that really freaked me out was when MacKenzie smirked at me and was all like, "Nikki, everyone in the entire school knows you're too CHICKEN to enter the art competition because I'M a better artist than you are. So don't bother!"

Okay. Even though MacKenzie didn't actually SAY those words to me, she definitely looked like she was THINKING them.

And, either way, it was a humongous INSULT to my integrity.

Then she kind of flipped her hair and sashayed out of the classroom. I just HATE it when MacKenzie sashays!

How DARE she talk about the art competition right to my face like that??!!

Especially when it was HER fault I DIDN'T enter to begin with.

This whole situation just TICKED me off!

Suddenly, I just totally lost it and screamed at the top of my lungs, "MacKenzie STARTED this WAR, and now I'M going to FINISH it!!"

But I said it in my head, so no one else heard it but me. Then I made a solemn promise to myself:

I, NIKKI J. MAXWELL,
being of sound mind and body,
am officially entering the
AVANT-GARDE ART
COMPETITION!!

I was going to show MacKenzie once and for all that I had MAD art skillz.

And MINE are

WAY MADDER

than HERS!

So I grabbed all my stuff and marched right down to the office to fill out an entry form.

Sure enough, MacKenzie was still in there, applying her fourteenth layer of lip gloss and bragging nonstop about her fashion illustrations.

". . . and everyone thinks my original designs are so HAWT, and I'm going to be RICH and FAMOUS and move to HOLLYWOOD and blah-blah, blah-blah, blah-blah, blah!"

I was just casually chilling out behind a big potted plant right outside the office door, minding my own business, when, FINALLY, MacKenzie left.

But it was NOT like I was spying on her or anything. I mean, like, how juvenile would THAT be. . . .

ME, JUST CHILLING OUT BEHIND A PLANT!

I just didn't want to attract a lot of attention to myself or have MacKenzie think I was making a big deal out of the fact that I was entering the competition.

Although, to be honest, it WAS a big deal.

It was THE most important thing I had EVER attempted in my entire fourteen years of life here on planet Earth.

I rushed into the office and quickly filled out an entry form.

As I handed it to the assistant, I felt a rush of panic, excitement, and nausea, all mixed up together, whirling around in my stomach like leftovers in a garbage disposal.

Or it might have been a bad case of indigestion from that NASTY Tuna Noodle Surprise I'd had for lunch.

I walked out of the office and collapsed against the wall. My heart was pounding so hard, I could hear it in my ears.

I began to wonder if this whole thing was a big mistake.

Then, out of the blue, I got a really creepy feeling

that someone was watching me, even though the halls seemed empty.

Suddenly, a leaf on the plant I had hidden behind moved, and I saw this EYE staring out at me! Then two eyes. Very icy blue ones.

OMG! MACKENZIE WAS SPYING ON ME!!

She was, like, SO BUSTED! Finally, MacKenzie climbed out from behind the plant and sashayed over to the drinking fountain like she was thirsty or something.

But it was very obvious to me that she was just trying to use WATER TORTURE to FORCE me to change my mind about entering the art competition.

"OOPSY! MY BAD!"

MacKenzie tried to act all innocent and apologetic, like the whole squirting me with water thing was just an accident. But I looked into her beady little eyes and could tell she absolutely meant to do it.

I still could not get over the fact that I had actually caught her SPYING on me!

Which kind of made me ANGRY, because I don't follow her around, SPYING on her and getting all up in her Kool-Aid (which, BTW, means "business").

Well, at least not that often.

Today was, like, *TOTALLY* an exception, mainly because we were both turning in entries for the art competition at the same time.

But to stoop so low as to SPY on me?!

THAT GIRL IS ONE SICK LITTLE PUPPY!

I ABSOLUTELY HATE! HATE! HATE! HATE! HATE! HATE! HATE! HATE! HATE! HATE! HATE! HATE!

THIS STUPID SCHOOL!!

Today at lunch, I was carrying my tray and trying to get to table 9, where I was supposed to meet Chloe and Zoey.

Things were going pretty good, because I had managed to sneak past the jock table without the football players making those embarrassing farting noises with their armpits.

But as I was walking past MacKenzie's table, I really wasn't paying attention. She must have STILL been pretty mad at me about the party invitation and the art competition, because this is what happened:

112

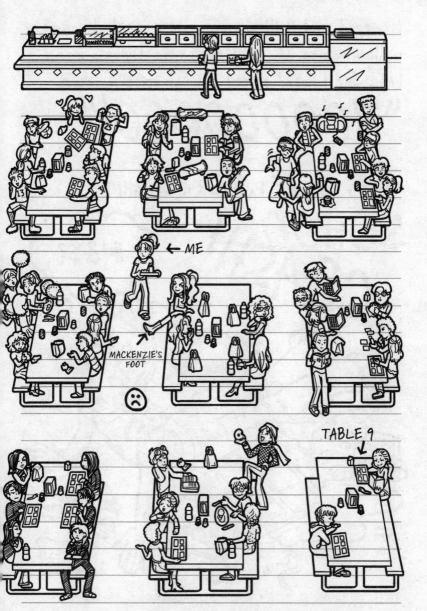

← ME

MACKENZIE'S FOOT

TABLE 9

ME, IN THE CAFETERIA, TRYING
TO GET TO TABLE 9!

I tripped, and suddenly, everything started moving in slow motion. My lunch tray went flying over my head, and I heard a very familiar voice shrieking,

"NOOOOOOOO!"

Then, in HORROR, I realized it was MINE! . . .

ME, TRIPPING AND DROPPING
MY LUNCH TRAY IN THE CAFETERIA

I fell flat on the floor and was so stunned, I could barely breathe.

My spaghetti and cherry jubilee dessert were smeared across my face and the front of my clothes. I looked like a life-size version of one of Brianna's messy finger paintings.

I just closed my eyes and lay there like a beached whale, with every inch of my body aching. Even my hair hurt.

However, the worst part was that the ENTIRE cafeteria was laughing like crazy.

I was SO embarrassed, I wanted to DISAPPEAR. I could barely see, because I had cherry jubilee in my eyes and it made everything look red and really blurry.

Finally, I gathered the strength to crawl to my knees.

But each time I tried to get up, I slipped in the mixture of spaghetti and milk and fell back down again.

I have to admit, I probably looked hilarious sloshing around in my lunch like that. Then MacKenzie folded her arms, glared at me, and said,

"SO, NIKKI, DID YOU HAVE A NICE TRIP?!"

Of course, that witty little comment made everyone laugh even harder.

It was the CRUELEST thing MacKenzie could have possibly said, especially since SHE was totally responsible for my "trip."

I was so humiliated, I started to cry.

The good news was, the tears washed all the gunk out of my eyes, and I could see again.

But the bad news was, all I could see was this guy kneeling over me with a camera dangling in my face.

And only ONE person in the whole entire school owns a camera like that.

I had no idea why my crush, Brandon, would want to permanently capture the most utterly humiliating moment in my entire pathetic life in a PHOTO.

Sorry, but I'm getting SUPERupset all over again just writing about all of this.

I think I need to go and have a good cry!

I'll finish this diary entry later.

Maybe . . .

☹!!

Okay, I'll try this again.

After I saw that camera in my face, I knew EXACTLY what was going to appear on the FRONT PAGE of the next issue of our school newspaper. . . .

ME ☹!!

It was very obvious to me that some way, somehow, MacKenzie had completely charmed Brandon with her awesome beautyliciousness and lured him over to the DARK SIDE! And then BRAINWASHED him!

How could my CRUSH—the secret LOVE of my life—do such a HORRIBLE and WICKED thing to me?!

I felt like I had been stabbed in the heart with my favorite lucky purple ink pen—the hot-pink sparkly one with the feathers, beads, and sequins on the end—by my beloved BRANDON!! And left to DIE. On the floor of the cafeteria. With everyone watching. And laughing.

Then the most bizarre thing happened!

Brandon kind of smiled at me, slid his camera out of the way, grabbed my hand, and pulled me up off the floor.

"Are you okay?" he asked.

I tried to say "Yes," but my voice just made a gurgling sound like I was strangling or something. I swallowed and took a deep breath.

"Sure. I'm fine. I had spaghetti for dinner yesterday, but it wasn't nearly this slippery!"

I cringed. I couldn't believe I just said that. I am SUCH an IDIOT!!

Then I watched, spellbound, as Brandon handed me a napkin in what seemed like slow motion. I almost FAINTED, right there on the spot, when our fingers accidentally TOUCHED . . .

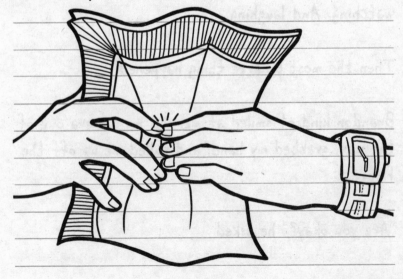

. . . ever so slightly, like a gentle but wild squirrel slurping sweet nectar from one of those dainty purply flowers in my mother's garden that my dad accidentally sprayed with weed killer. Our eyes locked, and for a split second, it was as if we were gazing into the deep, misty cavern of each other's wounded souls. I will FOREVER remember the words he whispered into my trembling ear:

"Um . . . I think you have . . . something on your face?"

I blushed and my knees started feeling all wobbly.

"Probably my lunch . . ."

"Yeah, probably . . ."

Unfortunately, our very serious emo convo (which means "emotional conversation") was rudely interrupted by Mr. Snodgrass, our lunchroom monitor. But everyone calls him Mr. Snot and a not-so-nice word.

He started cleaning up the mess on the floor and lecturing me about my responsibility as a young adult to keep my food on my tray at all times. Brandon rolled his eyes at Mr. Snodgrass in a very chivalrous manner, and then he kind of smiled at me again.

"I guess I'll see you in biology."

"Yeah . . . okay. And thanks. You know, for the napkin."

"Hey, no prob."

"Actually, we have napkins just like this at home. My mom got them at the store. . . ."

"Oh, that's, um . . . cool. Well, later."

"Sure, see you in bio."

Then Brandon picked up his backpack and left the cafeteria.

I just clutched the napkin over my heart and sighed.

In spite of everything that had just happened, I suddenly felt VERY happy and tingly all over.

But that feeling lasted only about ten seconds, because that's how long it took for MacKenzie to completely RUIN the moment.

NIKKI, DON'T GET YOUR HOPES UP. BRANDON WOULD NEVER LIKE A FREAK LIKE YOU!

I just stared at her. I could NOT believe that girl was talking trash like that right to my face.

Then MacKenzie blurted, "YOU are such a DORK! OMG! Look at her! I think she PEED her pants!"

And then Jessica said, "OMG! You're right. She did PEE her pants!"

Both of them pointed and laughed at me while the ENTIRE cafeteria watched.

I was about to have another MELTDOWN! So I ran out of the cafeteria and went straight to the girls' bathroom.

There were three girls in there at the mirror, trying out one another's lip gloss flavors. They completely froze and gawked at me in shock with their mouths dangling open.

It was like they had NEVER seen anyone covered from head to foot in spaghetti and cherry jubilee before.

Some people are so RUDE!

I kind of staggered back into the hallway like a zombie.

But instead of leaving a trail of slimy, rotted flesh, I left a trail of spaghetti, sauce, and cherry jubilee.

I was a DISGUSTING . . . EMBARRASSING . . .

MESS!!

I wanted to go hide inside my locker and stay there until the school year was over.

Why does it seem like almost everyone at this school HATES ME?!

!!

I can't believe I'm STILL writing about what MacKenzie did to me in the cafeteria on Tuesday.

That girl is such a

DRAMA QUEEN!!

I guess I must be

TRAUMATIZED

or something.

Anyway, I was seriously thinking about calling my mom and going home for the rest of the day. That's when I noticed the janitor's utility closet near the drinking fountain.

I tried the door and was relieved when it actually opened. I checked over my shoulder to make sure no one was watching me.

Then I snuck inside. . . .

Alone at last.

With a mildewy mop.

I closed my eyes and sighed deeply.

OMG!! I felt just AWFUL! I burst into tears and started writing in my diary.

Pretty soon I heard some vaguely familiar voices whispering and snickering outside the door.

I just knew MacKenzie and her crew were looking for me to harass me some more about peeing my pants.

"Are you sure she's in there?"

"I think so. The spaghetti leads right up to this door and stops."

"You're right. Look at these cherry jubilee footprints! She HAS to be hiding in there."

I was like, JUST GREAT ☹!!

At that moment I would have given anything to just DISAPPEAR into thin air.

Then they actually had the nerve to knock on my door. Well, not exactly MY door, but the door to the janitor's closet.

I felt like the victim in one of those horror movies where the girl is home alone and hears a knock at the front door.

And when she goes to open the door, everyone in the audience is yelling, "DON'T OPEN IT! DON'T OPEN IT!"

But she opens the door anyway because she doesn't KNOW she's in a HORROR MOVIE.

Sorry, but I WASN'T that stupid! I KNEW I was trapped in a horror flick, so I DIDN'T open the door to the janitor's closet.

All of a sudden it got really quiet, and I suspected it was a trick to make me think they had left.

But I had a feeling in my gut they were still out there.

"Nikki, are you okay?! We just heard what happened."

"Yeah, we wanted to make sure you were all right!"

That's when I finally recognized the voices.

It was CHLOE and ZOEY!!

Zoey said, "Girl, don't make me bust this door down, because you know I will do it!"

That kind of made me laugh, because Zoey has trouble opening her locker. And sometimes even her bottled water.

I was like, *Yeah, right!*

Then Chloe said, "If you're not going to come out and talk to us, we're coming IN!"

The next thing I knew, Chloe and Zoey were poking their heads inside the janitor's closet and acting all goofy. Chloe was snorting and giving me "jazz hands," and Zoey was sticking out her tongue and giving me the "stink eye."

They were like . . .

"WHAT'S UP, GIRLFRIEND!!"

For some reason, seeing them made me start crying all over again. Soon the three of us were just chilling out in the janitor's closet talking about all the drama with MacKenzie and Jessica. . . .

CHLOE, ZOEY, AND ME, JUST CHILLING OUT
IN THE JANITOR'S CLOSET

But I left out the part about Brandon on purpose, because I was still kind of embarrassed about it.

Plus, I was pretty sure he'd pick MacKenzie over me any day. If I were a guy, I sure would.

I was so NOT getting my hopes up about Brandon actually liking me.

Pretty soon the lunch period was almost over. Chloe and Zoey helped scrub most of the food stains off my clothes with paper towels and hand soap right at the big sink.

There were still some stains we couldn't get off, though. I couldn't believe it when Zoey ran to her locker to get me her favorite lucky sweater to wear to cover them up.

And Chloe said that if I applied an extra amount of her Candy Apple Swirl ultrashiny lip gloss along with her midnight blue eyeliner, everyone (especially the guys) would notice my beautiful luscious lips and dreamy eyes instead of the pea stain . . . er . . . I mean, MILK stain on the front of my pants.

Which, lucky for me, was not that noticeable, since it had started to dry up.

Anyway, in spite of how bad things were at lunch on Tuesday, Chloe and Zoey definitely made me feel a lot better.

They're the BEST friends EVER ☺!!

I guess maybe I don't hate this school quite as much anymore.

But I bet Brandon thinks I'm a

TOTAL KLUTZ!!
☹!

I was up and getting ready for school when I noticed I had a HUGE pimple right on my cheek. . . .

I almost CHOKED on my minty-fresh, tartar control, extra-brightening, mouthwash-strength, cavity-fighting gel toothpaste!

Sorry!

But now that my crush, Brandon, had FINALLY noticed I was alive, there was NO WAY I was going to school completely disfigured like that.

And I was NOT looking forward to MacKenzie getting all up in my personal business by making nasty little comments disguised as "invaluable advice," like . . .

"OMG, Nikki!! You have a HUGE ZIT on your cheek! But here's some invaluable advice. If you don't have any concealer, I suggest you try covering it up with your extra-long nose hairs!"

Anyway, I knew my mom was NOT going to let me stay home from school unless I was spiking a temperature of at least 289 degrees.

Which, BTW, is the same temp she uses to bake her
Thanksgiving turkey. . . .

289°

MOM'S TEMPERATURE REQUIREMENTS
FOR A THANKSGIVING TURKEY <u>AND</u>
A SICK DAUGHTER

My mom's life motto is "Hey! Why let a little case
of gangrene or leprosy get in the way of achieving
a good education?!"

After trying every trick in the book, I FINALLY figured out how to convince my mom I was too ill to go to school.

I had to PRETEND to throw up all over myself. Now, how SICK is THAT?!

I came up with this idea last spring after Brianna had the stomach flu.

Mom took time off from work and let my little sister stay home from school for an entire week.

On top of that, she totally pampered Brianna by buying her all of her favorite Disney movies and a new Princess Sugar Plum computer game to keep her occupied while she was in bed.

I think all that vomiting must have really gotten to Mom. About three weeks later, I stayed home from school with a bad case of strep throat and was hoping to at least get a couple of presents out of it.

But all Mom bought me was a cruddy box of Popsicles!

And, to make matters worse, they were the really gross low-calorie kind with no sugar.

They tasted like frozen pickle juice on a stick.

I was like . . .

DELISH!

☹

Thanks a million, Mom!

But I have to admit, Brianna WAS a lot sicker than I was.

She couldn't keep anything down, not even water!

I refused to go anywhere near her unless I was suited up in full "puke protection" gear. . . .

ME, READY FOR BRIANNA'S PROJECTILE
VOMITING DUE TO HER STOMACH FLU! YUCK!

Since I was pretty sure Mom was not going to
consider my pimple serious enough to let me stay
home from school, I decided to run downstairs and
make a quick batch of phony vomit.

Lucky for me, I was the first one out of bed, which meant I had the kitchen completely to myself for about fifteen minutes.

Since things were going to get a little messy, I changed into my old heart pj's and rushed downstairs. My secret recipe was easy to make, and it looked and smelled like the real thing:

STAY-HOME-FROM-SCHOOL PHONY VOMIT

1 cup of cooked oatmeal

½ cup of sour cream (or buttermilk ranch dressing or anything that smells like rancid, sour milk)

2 chopped cheese sticks (for chunkiness)

1 uncooked egg (for authentic slimy texture)

1 can of split pea soup (for putrid green color)

¼ cup of raisins (to increase gross-osity)

Mix ingredients and simmer over low heat for 2 minutes. Let mixture cool to warm vomit temperature. Use liberally as needed. Makes 4 to 5 cups.

WARNING: This stuff is SO gross that it might REALLY make you sick to your stomach and cause you to REALLY throw up. In which case, you will REALLY need to stay home from school ☹!

I poured about 2 cups into a bowl, ran back upstairs to my room, and dumped it down the front of my heart pj's.

Then I yelled down the hall in a really whiny voice:

"MOM! Please come quick! I don't feel so good. My stomach is really queasy and I think I'm going to . . .

blecchuuarggh!"

(That was the sound of me throwing up!)

Of course it worked like a charm ☺!!

Mom was totally convinced. She said that although I had an upset stomach, I was not running a temperature, and I'd probably feel better after a day of bed rest.

I told her that suddenly I was feeling a lot better already (wink wink). Then she cleaned up my "mess," helped with my bubble bath, and tucked me back into bed with a kiss.

I actually slept until noon! However, when I went into the kitchen to grab a bite for lunch, I suddenly realized I had completely FORGOTTEN to pour the leftovers of my phony vomit down the garbage disposal!

JUST GREAT ☹!!

I need to ADD one final, important step to that recipe:

DISPOSE OF ALL THE INCRIMINATING EVIDENCE!

So when I saw that my mom had left a note for me on the counter right next to the now empty pot of puke, I just KNEW she was onto me and I was in really BIG trouble.

I totally panicked and my stomach started feeling queasy, but this time FOR REAL!

Her note said:

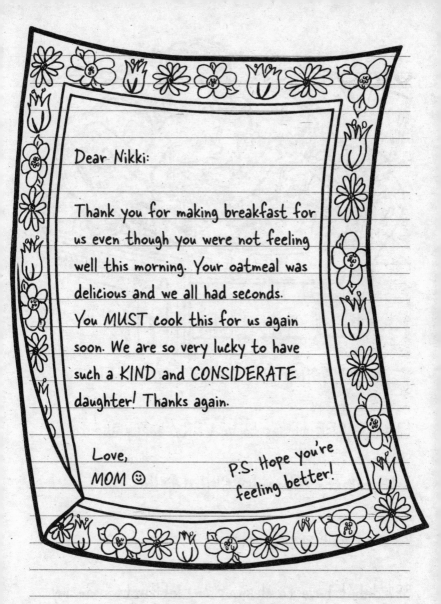

Dear Nikki:

Thank you for making breakfast for us even though you were not feeling well this morning. Your oatmeal was delicious and we all had seconds. You MUST cook this for us again soon. We are so very lucky to have such a KIND and CONSIDERATE daughter! Thanks again.

Love,
MOM ☺

P.S. Hope you're feeling better!

I spent the entire afternoon just lounging around, watching television, and raiding the fridge. I even ordered a pizza! . . .

ME, PIGGING OUT WHILE I WATCHED TV!

I had THREE things to be VERY happy about:

1. I spent the entire day CHILLAXING.

2. My pimple pretty much cleared up.

3. I didn't have to clean up any leftovers from my pot of puke because my family ATE it.

SQUEEEEEE!! ☺!!

I think I'm suffering from Nomophobia.

I know it sounds like some really nasty disease where you're covered from head to toe with itchy, runny sores, or something hideous like that.

But it's actually the IRRATIONAL fear of NOT having a cell phone.

The worst thing about Nomophobia is that it sometimes causes hallucinations and makes you do insanely STUPID things.

I think I had an attack of this very debilitating disease when I went outside to get the mail.

I thought for sure I saw a tiny, cute cell phone thingy that clips around your ear lying on the sidewalk near our mailbox.

I was like, SWEET!! A FREE phone thingy! It's ALL GOOD!

But when I took a closer look, it was kind of a bright peachy color. I guessed that what I had found was actually a HEARING AID.

Of course, I was devastated when I finally figured this out, because I was really pumped about having found a free phone thingy just lying there on the sidewalk.

I figured it probably belonged to Mrs. Wallabanger, the nice old lady who lives next door.

I suspect she is hard of hearing because whenever I say "Good morning" to her, she answers with something random like "Thank you, dear! I got them for only $1.50 at Bertha's yard sale!"

My mom says she has two grandsons who are the same ages as Brianna and me, but I haven't met them yet.

She also has a scrawny little Yorkie named Creampuff. He looks like a cute, fuzzy ball of lint with four paws, but he's as vicious as a Doberman. . . .

CREAMPUFF IS SUPERCUTE,
BUT HE HATES EVERYONE.

Anyway, I wanted to ask Mrs. Wallabanger if she had lost her hearing aid.

I figured if she HADN'T, it would be a waste of my time and energy.

And if she HAD, it would be an EVEN BIGGER waste of my time and energy. I was right. This is what happened. . . .

ME, TALKING TO MRS. WALLABANGER, BUT SHE CAN'T HEAR ME.

WHAT I SAID	WHAT SHE SAID
Hi, Mrs. Wallabanger. I just stopped by to ask if you lost your hearing aid?	What did you say, missy?
Your HEARING AID!! Is it lost?	Eh? Speak up, why don't cha?
Did you lose your HEARING AID?!	Eh? You say, I need to lose my HAIRY LEGS . . . ?!!
HEARING AID!! HEARING AID!!	Don't get fresh with me, you little whippersnapper!! My HAIRY LEGS are NONE of your BEESWAX. GET OFF MY PROPERTY!!

My little chat with Mrs. Wallabanger did NOT go well. After she very rudely kicked me out of her yard, I just stuck the hearing aid inside her mailbox and hoped that she'd find it in there at some point.

Since she only comes out of her house to walk her dog, what's the WORST that could happen?! . . .

Okay, so maybe the WORST that could happen is Mrs. Wallabanger gets run over by a semitruck! But could you really say it was MY fault?! ☹!!

Since I wanted her to stay safe, I decided the moral and right thing to do was to just GIVE the hearing aid back to her.

ANONYMOUSLY!

I took it out of her mailbox and put it in a little gift box with a bow on it and attached a note. . . .

To:
Mrs.
Wallabanger 😊

Then I placed it on her front step, rang her doorbell, and ran away.

It's not like I was SCARED of her or anything. I just wanted it to be a surprise.

Later that evening, I saw Mrs. Wallabanger walking her dog and, sure enough, she was wearing her hearing aid and a HUGE smile.

I waved at her and said, "I hope you and Creampuff have a nice walk!"

"Well, I always use Ex-Lax for MY constipation, so it might work for you, too!" she answered.

So now I'm thinking she has trouble with her hearing AND her MEMORY!

Because she obviously FORGOT to turn on her hearing aid!

I'm thinking she and my grandma could probably be BFFs!

☺!!

I think Chloe and Zoey have totally lost their minds!

They practically FREAKED OUT when Mrs. Peach announced she was taking six of her most hardworking and committed LSAs on a five-day field trip to the New York City Public Library to participate in National Library Week.

Mrs. Peach is already making plans, even though it's in April, which is still a whole seven months away. From what I understand, it's like a big Mardi Gras celebration for people obsessed with libraries.

Chloe and Zoey actually started jumping up and down and screaming.

I was like, "Girlfriends, take a chill pill,

PUH-LEEZE!"

But I just said that inside my head, so no one else heard it but me.

The whole time we were shelving books, they were talking nonstop about how we needed to do something really special to convince Mrs. Peach to select the three of us for the trip to NYC.

"Well, why don't we just try to be the MOST hardworking and committed LSAs?" I suggested. "And we could start by maybe dusting off the books."

It was a no-brainer to me.

But Chloe and Zoey both looked at me like I was crazy.

"ALL of the other LSAs are going to be doing boring stuff like THAT to impress her!" Chloe groaned.

"Yeah! We need to come up with a secret plan that will blow Mrs. Peach's mind!" Zoey said excitedly.

Okay, so dusting the library books was NOT exactly a mind-blowing idea. But it definitely would have solved my little sneezing problem.

We were putting out a batch of brand-new magazines when Chloe swiped a *That's So Hot!* and buried her nose in it. Suddenly, she gasped and then shrieked. . . .

OMG! ZOEY AND NIKKI, THIS IS *EXACTLY* WHAT WE SHOULD DO!!

CHLOE GOOFING OFF WHILE
ZOEY AND I WORK

"What? Get makeovers and become teen SUPERMODELS?" I asked sarcastically.

"NO! Of course not!" Chloe answered.

"I know! We should MAKE. YOUR. FACE. ZIT. PROOF!" Zoey said, reading an ad for Zap-It acne cream over Chloe's shoulder.

"Zoey, are you KA-RAY-ZEE?!" Chloe exclaimed. "No! Just . . . NO!"

I decided to guess again.

"We should, um, publish our OWN magazine so that we can give teens all over the world advice on fashion, fun, friends, flirting, guys, and love, so THEIR lives won't be as disgustingly CRUDDY as OURS?!"

Chloe just gave me a GIGANTIC eye roll.

Then she flipped over the magazine and pointed at an article. . . .

"I think a TATTOO promoting READING would be PERFECT! And it would show that we're serious and committed. Then Mrs. Peach will choose us for the field trip for sure!" Chloe squealed excitedly.

"That's a WICKED idea!" Zoey said, staring in awe at the beautiful, tattooed model in the magazine. "I bet we're going to look as cool as her once we get ours! SWEET!"

Okay. Hanging out in New York City for National Library Week sounded like a lot of fun.

But there was just NO WAY I was going to try to earn that trip by getting a tattoo to celebrate reading!

I mean, WHAT kind of tattoo would I even get? . . .

READ

OR DIE!!

I had to think fast. "Um . . . I agree this is the coolest idea EVER, you guys. But I just found out a few days ago that I might be . . . um . . . ALLERGIC to certain types of . . . ink. So I have to be really careful about what type of artist ink I use. Which means I'm probably allergic to, um, tattoo ink as well."

Chloe and Zoey looked a little confused.

"Well, I would imagine that artist ink and tattoo ink are very different. And you being allergic to them BOTH just sounds very . . . bizarre," Chloe said, narrowing her eyes at me skeptically, like I was lying to her or something.

Zoey agreed. That's when I lost it and yelled at them both, "You know what I think is BIZARRE? Bizarre is getting a

TATTOO

for National Library Week!!"

But I just said that inside my head, so no one else heard it but me. "Well, bizarre or not, I'm pretty sure I'm allergic," I insisted. "Which is really unfair because I was totally looking forward to getting a tattoo one day before I die."

Then I sniffed a few times like I was very upset and emotionally distraught over NOT being able to get a tattoo.

"Nikki, if it's a medical problem, we completely understand. Right, Zoey?" Chloe was trying to make me feel better. "Hey! Why don't you help us pick out OUR tattoos?"

"Yeah, we should ask our parents to take us to get them this weekend!" Zoey said excitedly. "I can hardly wait to see the look on Mrs. Peach's face when she sees our tattoos!"

But I already knew what her face was going to look like when she saw Chloe and Zoey covered with tattoos that celebrate reading. . . .

I was hoping Chloe and Zoey were finally over their totally wacky idea of getting tattoos for National Library Week.

Thank goodness their parents said "No way!"

But when I saw them in PE class, they were still pretty upset.

Our PE teacher divided us up into groups of three for our ballet skills test, and at first, I was happy that Chloe, and Zoey, and I were together.

Each group was supposed to pick classical music from the teacher's CD collection and then make up a short dance routine using the five ballet positions we had learned over the past weeks.

Since I knew all of them, I was sure I was going to get an A or, at lowest, maybe a B+ on the test.

ME, DEMONSTRATING MY AWESOME
BALLET TECHNIQUE

But, unfortunately, Chloe and Zoey were too miserable to participate.

I was like, "Come on, guys, cheer up! We have to make up our ballet routine and practice it before we run out of time." But both of them just stared at me with big sad puppy-dog eyes.

"I can't believe our parents aren't letting us get tattoos! How unfair is that?" Chloe whined.

"And now Mrs. Peach will NEVER pick us for the trip to NYC! It's like our hopes and dreams have shriveled up and DIED!" Zoey sniffed, wiping a tear.

They spent the next forty-five minutes venting, and I, being the sensitive and caring friend that I am, sat quietly and listened. Then the PE teacher came over and told us she was ready to start grading and we were going to be the second group to go.

I just about had a heart attack because we hadn't picked any music or made up a routine.

I ran over really quick to grab a CD, and the only one left was *Swan Lake*.

And since I had seen MacKenzie looking at it a few minutes earlier, I was definitely a little suspicious.

So the first thing I did was pop open the CD case and peek inside.

I was surprised and relieved to see that a CD was still in there.

Hey, I didn't trust that girl as far as I could throw her.

MacKenzie's group was first, and I have to admit, they were pretty good. But it wasn't due to their awesome talent.

Combined, the three of them had, like, eighty-nine years of private lessons.

They danced to "Dance of the Sugar Plum Fairy" and ended their routine like this. . . .

MACKENZIE'S BALLET GROUP

What a bunch of **SHOW-OFFS!**

I mean, what real classically trained ballerina would end her dance by doing splits and smiling like she just got her braces off or something?

I was like, "Hey, girlfriends! This AIN'T that cheesy TV show *Dancing with the Stars!*" But I just said it inside my head, so no one else heard it but me.

We were up next, and I started getting butterflies in my stomach. Not because I was nervous. I just really hated humiliating myself in public.

Chloe must have seen the look on my face because she whispered, "Don't panic! Just follow my lead. I took ballet lessons for three weeks back in second grade!"

I said, "Thanks for sharing that, Chloe. Now I feel SO much better!" ☹

Then Zoey whispered, "What lies behind us and what lies before us are tiny matters compared to what lies within us. Ralph Waldo Emerson." Which, of course, had NOTHING WHATSOEVER to do with ANYTHING!

I had a really bad feeling about our routine, and we hadn't even started it yet.

Mainly because I discovered our Swan Lake CD was actually NOT a Swan Lake CD. It said Swan Lake on the case, but the CD inside said something else.

170

When I read the title, I was like . . .

It was *Thriller* by Michael Jackson!

Then my teacher snatched the CD out of my hand and popped it into her CD player and told us to take our places in front of the class.

I was about to explain that we had a slight complication with our music, but I got distracted when MacKenzie's group started squealing and hugging each other.

They had gotten an A+ on their routine.

But it was not like I was jealous or anything. I mean, how totally juvenile would THAT be?

Anyway, when our music came on, Chloe must have completely forgotten we were supposed to be doing a ballet routine, because she started doing some funky dance moves like she was one of those half-rotted zombies from the "Thriller" music video.

The next thing I knew, Zoey was acting like a zombie too, so I didn't have a choice but to follow along.

Plus, I figured our teacher would probably knock a few points off our grade if Chloe and Zoey were staggering around like the undead and

I was doing ballet pliés in first and third positions.

Okay. I really, really like Chloe and Zoey.

But while I was up there dancing with them, I couldn't help thinking, What am I? Flypaper for FREAKS?!

I had to keep reminding myself that this whole thing was MacKenzie's fault, not THEIRS.

Chloe, Zoey, and me performing . . .

BALLET

OF THE

ZOMBIES!!

Actually, I was surprised that Chloe and Zoey were such good dancers.

It looked like our PE teacher was pretty impressed too, because when we finished, she just stared at us with her mouth open and started tapping her ink pen on her clipboard really fast.

Then she asked us to see her after class.

We were really nervous when we went up to talk to her, because we didn't know what to expect.

Chloe and Zoey thought maybe she was going to ask us to join the school's dance squad, since she is the assistant coach. I was keeping my fingers crossed on that one.

I'd heard that the dance squad members were pretty much known as PARTY ANIMALS!

So this opportunity could help to improve my very lame rep as a socially challenged DORK! I know, right ☺?!

Our teacher smiled and said, "Girls, if we were doing the section on contemporary dance, you would have definitely gotten an A+!"

After hearing that, I was pretty sure she was going to give us a good grade on our routine even though we had made it up on the spot and with the wrong music.

Then our teacher stopped smiling.

"The three of you were supposed to be doing classical ballet, but you weren't even close. The highest grade I can give you is a D. I'm really sorry."

We were like,

OH. NO. SHE. DIDN'T!!

Chloe, Zoey, and I were literally

CRUSHED!

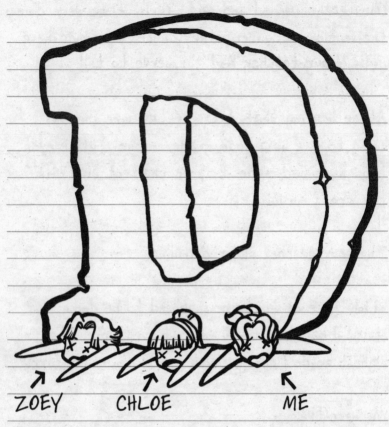

ZOEY   CHLOE   ME

Then I screamed at my teacher, "Are you NUTS?!
How in the world can you give us a D? Do you even
realize how tricky those dance steps were? It was
definitely A LOT harder than it looked! Let me see
YOU try to moonwalk like a zombie, sister!"

But I just said all of that in my head, so no one
heard it but me.

And get this!

THEN our teacher had the nerve to tell us to "hit the showers"! Like, what did showering have to do with classical ballet?!

ABSOLUTELY NOTHING!!

I was a little peeved at Chloe and Zoey, because if they had NOT been wasting time whining about tattoos and National Library Week, we could have made up a decent ballet routine to the correct music and maybe earned at least a C.

But NOOOOOO!

THEN, at lunch, things went from bad to worse. Chloe and Zoey had a

TOTAL MELTDOWN!

179

They actually came up with this elaborate scheme to run away from home and live in the secret underground tunnels beneath the New York City Public Library!

But the crazy part was that they planned to leave this Friday and then just "hang out" for seven whole months until National Library Week rolled around in April.

They figured that, by arriving early, they'd get in

FREE.

Chloe said residing at the library was going to be an "exhilarating experience" because they could read all the books they wanted, twenty-four hours a day, without having to check them out or reshelve them.

And Zoey said they were going to live off Diet Pepsi and nachos, which they planned to SWIPE from the library snack bar each night! . . .

CHLOE AND ZOEY, USING THEIR NATURAL
INSTINCTS TO SCAVENGE FOR FOOD

I CANNOT believe Chloe and Zoey are actually going
to do something so crazy, dangerous, and illegal.

And I plan to do everything within my power to
STOP them!

WHY?!

Because Chloe and Zoey are my BEST friends at this school!

And my ONLY friends at this school! But that's beside the point.

Unfortunately, I only have TWO options:

1. Rat them out to their parents and risk losing their friendship forever

OR

2. Figure out a way to get girlfriends some tattoos for National Library Week PDQ (which, BTW, means "pretty darn quick")!!

I hardly got any sleep last night! I kept having horrible nightmares about Chloe and Zoey living in the secret underground tunnels beneath the NYC public library. . . .

In one of my dreams, they were having a dinner party with some of their neighbors.

And in the scariest one, I got married to Brandon, and Chloe and Zoey were bridesmaids. But they brought a few uninvited guests to my wedding ☹! . . .

I actually woke up SCREAMING my head off until I realized it was all just a very bad dream!

This morning at breakfast, Brianna got on my last nerve.

I was just sitting there, eating my Cap'n Crunch, reading the back of the cereal box, and trying to figure out what I was going to do about the Chloe and Zoey situation.

They were planning to leave in less than twenty-four hours.

Brianna was eating Fruity Pebbles and drawing a face on her hand with an ink pen. She said she was naming the face "Miss Penelope" because she was "borned from a pen."

BRIANNA'S HAND

Even though I was trying to concentrate on my personal problems, Miss Penelope asked me to watch her perform "Itsy-Bitsy Spider," the Princess Sugar Plum rock remix.

The whole thing was totally annoying, because I'm not that into puppet shows. . . .

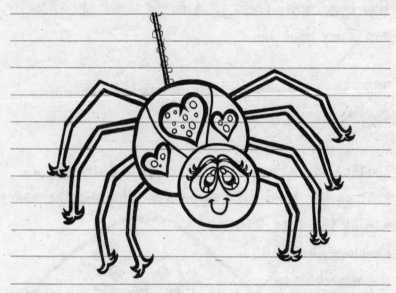

Anyway, I warned both Brianna and Miss Penelope to quit bothering me, mainly because I was in a really HORRIBLE MOOD.

And it was not helping matters that Miss Penelope's awful singing sounded like a humpback whale in labor.

She must have been highly insulted by my unbiased critique of her singing abilities, because she hauled off and socked me on my arm.

So I grabbed Miss Penelope and shoved her headfirst right into my cereal bowl.

I was like, "Got milk?!" . . .

ME, TRYING TO DROWN MISS PENELOPE
IN MY BOWL OF CEREAL!!

Brianna started screaming, "Stop it! Miss Penelope can't swim! Let her go! You're smushing her face!"

But I wouldn't let go.

That is, until my mom walked into the kitchen.

"NIKKI MAXWELL! Why on earth are you shoving your sister's hand in your cereal?! LET GO OF HER THIS INSTANT!!"

So I released Miss Penelope only because I didn't have a choice.

Brianna stuck her tongue out at me. "Miss Penelope says she's not inviting you to her birthday party! Na, na—na, na, na!!"

Then I stuck my tongue out at HER and said, "Sorry, but I've ALREADY not been invited to a birthday party. SO THERE!"

I could thank MacKenzie for that one.

Anyway, I think I taught Miss Penelope a good lesson. I bet she won't be interrupting my breakfast again anytime soon (EVIL GRIN).

Since my cereal had been contaminated by Miss Penelope's germs, I dumped it into the sink and ran upstairs to my bedroom.

I sat on my bed and stared at my pencil cup as a million thoughts bounced around in my head.

I had to admit, the Chloe and Zoey situation seemed hopeless, and there was nothing I could do to fix it ☹.

To make matters worse, Miss Penelope was still in the kitchen singing so off-key, I thought my ears were going to bleed.

I felt like taking my favorite lucky pen—a water-based, nontoxic, dark purple gel ink pen by HotWriter, Inc.—and drawing a big fat zipper across her mouth to shut her up. . . .

MY LUCKY PEN

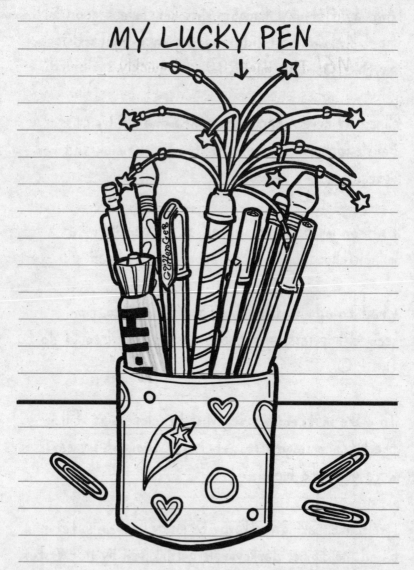

I mainly just use it to write in my diary and to bring me good luck. But lately, the good luck part hasn't been working so well.

I was twirling my pen in my fingers when, suddenly, the CRAZIEST idea popped into my head! I was like, OMG! This might work! I quickly scribbled out two notes and then rushed off to school fifteen minutes early to tape them on Chloe's and Zoey's lockers.

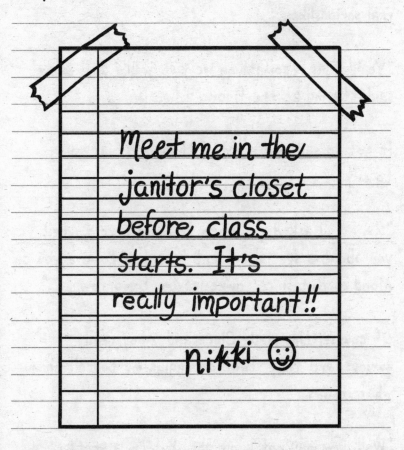

MY NOTE TO CHLOE AND ZOEY

I waited in the janitor's closet for five long minutes and was starting to worry they were not going to show up. But finally they did.

"I hope you didn't ask us to come here to try and change our minds about running away," Chloe said, real seriouslike.

"Yeah! This is something we just gotta do," Zoey said, staring at the floor.

It got so sad and quiet, I thought I was going to cry.

"Um . . . I asked you both to come here to tell you about a special present I wanted to give you on Monday. But since you're leaving tomorrow . . ."

Of course, this made Chloe and Zoey really curious, and they started begging me to tell them what it was.

"Well, you may not know this, but I'm a pretty decent artist. Not that I'm bragging or anything.

192

And since you guys are my BFFs, I've decided to personally give you each a tattoo! Temporary ones. In honor of National Library Week!"

At first Chloe and Zoey just stared at me like they couldn't believe it.

Then they started screaming and jumping up and down and hugging me.

ME, CHLOE, AND ZOEY, DOING A GROUP HUG!

"Just decide what kind you want," I said, "and I'll design it over the weekend and draw it during lunch on Monday. But you both have to make me one promise. . . ."

"Anything!!" Zoey gushed. "Let me guess! We have to ditch our plans to run away and live at the NYC library?"

"YEP! You got THAT right!" I exclaimed.

"Okay, then it's officially CANCELED!" Chloe announced, and did jazz hands, like the show was over.

"And there's another REALLY important thing I need to mention," I added, hiding my smile and trying to look all scary-serious. "I want you both to PROMISE me you WON'T bring RATS to my wedding, okay?"

"HUH?!" They both looked at me like I was crazy.

"Never mind!" I giggled. "It's a LOOONG story!" ☺!!

Before biology class started, I noticed Brandon was kind of staring at me, but I wasn't sure if it was my imagination or not. Lately, it seemed like whenever I looked at *HIM*, he was looking at *ME*.

Well, today he actually smiled at me and said, "So, which cell cycle would you rather study? Mitosis or meiosis?"

I smiled back and kind of shrugged my shoulders because I DISLIKED both of them EQUALLY. And I was afraid that anything I said would probably make me look like a BIGGER idiot than he already thought I was.

But the main reason I couldn't talk to Brandon was because I was suffering from a very severe and debilitating case of RCS, or Roller-Coaster Syndrome. Studies show that it mainly attacks girls between the ages of eight and sixteen.

The symptoms are difficult to describe, but

whenever Brandon talks to me, my stomach feels like I'm dropping nine hundred feet at eighty miles per hour. Simply calling it "butterflies" is a common and dangerous misdiagnosis.

Suddenly, and without warning, I feel compelled to throw my hands up in the air (like I just don't care) and scream . . .

"WHEEEEEE!"

I so LOVE to HATE this feeling ☺!!

ME, RIDING THE LOVE ROLLER COASTER!

Then my day got even BETTER!

While I was working in the library, Brandon came in to return a book called *Photography and You.*

I was just sitting there, doodling a few tattoo designs for Chloe and Zoey, when he leaned across the counter and peeked at my notebook.

"Now, THAT is good! I didn't know you were an artist!"

I looked around to see who he was talking to.

Then I totally freaked out when I realized he was actually talking to ME!

I could hardly BREATHE.

"Thanks, but it's no big deal. I've been going to art camp, like, forever. And last summer, I got practically a million mosquito bites and wow, did they ever itch!!" I babbled like an idiot.

"Well, one thing is for sure, you definitely got skillz!"

197

Brandon's hair was hanging in his eyes as he smiled and kind of leaned in even closer to look at my sketches.

I thought I was going to DIE!

He smelled like Snuggle fabric softener, Axe body spray, and . . . red licorice?!

I couldn't stop blushing, and there was no way I could draw with him watching me like that. I started feeling that roller-coaster thing all over again. . . .

WHEEEEE!

Then his face lit up.

"Hey! Are you entering the avant-garde art competition? I'll be covering it for the newspaper."

"Yeah, I'm thinking about it. But everyone is saying MacKenzie's fashion illustrations are going to win this year. So I don't know. . . ."

"MacKenzie?! Are you kidding? You have more talent in your smallest burp than she has in her entire body. I'm serious! You know that, right?"

I could NOT believe Brandon actually said that!

It was so rude. So wickedly funny.

So . . .

TRUE!

We both laughed really hard. I didn't know he had such a wacky sense of humor.

Soon Chloe and Zoey came staggering up to the front desk, each loaded down with a stack of books that needed to be put away.

When they saw us, their mouths dropped open.

They looked at me, then at Brandon, then at me again. Then at Brandon. Then back at me. Then Brandon. Then me. Then Brandon again.

This went on, like,

FOREVER!

They were gawking at us like we were a new animal
exhibit at the city ZOO or something. . . .

"HEY, CHECK OUT THOSE TWO! IT MUST BE
MATING SEASON OR SOMETHING. . . ."

It was SO embarrassing!

Brandon's smile went slightly crooked, but otherwise, he acted coolly nonchalant about the whole thing.

"Hey, Chloe! Hey, Zoey!" Brandon said, waving.

But they were so shocked, they didn't even answer him.

"Well, I'd better get back to class. See you later, Nikki." Then he strolled out the door and disappeared into the hall.

Chloe and Zoey made a big deal over Brandon talking to me like that and started nagging me to admit he was my secret crush.

After I made them both pinkie swear not to tell anyone, I told them about how Brandon had helped me up after MacKenzie tripped me in the cafeteria ten days ago.

Then I grabbed my backpack and unzipped the cute little pocket in the front and showed them The Napkin.

At first they just stared at it in awe.

But soon they were teasing me and giggling like two kindergarteners.

"Brandon and Nikki, sittin' in a tree,

K-I-S-S-I-N-G!"

I told them to shut up before someone overheard them and it got out all over the school.

Chloe insisted that I keep The Napkin for the rest of my life, because there was a chance that Brandon and I could accidentally meet up on some lush, exotic island twenty years from now.

She said it could happen just like it did in those romantic comedies at the movie theater. . . .

My Best Friend's Napkin

Directed by Chloe Christina Garcia

BRANDON:

I couldn't help but notice you from across the room and be hopelessly drawn to your brains and beauty! It almost seems that we've met before. Perhaps in another place . . . another time . . . another life . . . !

AHH–AHH! . . .

ME:

Alas! Allergy season is upon us. Please! Take this most cherished napkin from my very heart-wrenching, mysterious past. And do with it . . . what you must!!

ME:

What a powerful sneeze you have! It is aptly captured in this delicate napkin of forgotten love . . . now merely a disposable tissue drenched in lost and shattered dreams!

BRANDON:

Hark! Do mine eyes deceive me?! I'd recognize OUR napkin in even the darkest of murky depths! My joy and passion overwhelm me!

BRANDON:

Is it really you? My beloved, NIKKI! Finally, I've found my TRUE LOVE! Will you MARRY ME?!

ME:

Brandon, I've waited for this moment forever! Well, since middle school, anyway!

My answer is YES! A million times, YES!!

AND THEN WE LIVED HAPPILY EVER AFTER!!

THE END

I told Chloe her story was really sweet and romantic.

But if The Napkin was really dripping with snot and Brandon proposed on the spot like that, MY story would probably have a different ending. . . .

ME:
Gee, Brandon, I think we need to take things a bit slower. First, let's get rid of the snotty napkin . . . EWW!! Second, how about pizza and a movie . . . ?

THE END

Zoey said she didn't blame me for rewriting Chloe's happy ending, because snot and airborne bacterial particles were highly contagious and the most common way of transmitting germs to others.

But Chloe complained we both TOTALLY missed her point.

The Napkin, germy or not, should be cherished because it was a token of Brandon's love.

And after reading hundreds of teen romance novels, she had learned that forbidden love, obsession, and sacrifice could be very messy things. Just like snot.

I had to admit that Chloe had a really good point.

I'm just really glad Chloe and Zoey know so much about guys, dating, love, and stuff like that.

Because I don't have a CLUE.

DUH!!

☺!!

This is going to be my LONGEST diary entry EVER!

I have the most horrible headache, and it's all Brianna's fault.

Why, why, why couldn't I have been born an ONLY child?!

Okay. This is what happened: My mom and Brianna were supposed to see a matinee movie today.

But Mom needed to go to the mall to buy a present for a baby shower she was attending later this evening.

So she offered me $10 to take Brianna to the movie in her place. Since I was broke, I agreed to do it. I figured that, at the worst, I could sleep through the movie and earn $10 for a ninety-minute nap.

The movie was called *Princess Sugar Plum Saves Baby Unicorn Island! Part 3*.

There must have been four hundred squealing little girls there, and half of them were dressed up like princesses and unicorns.

I should have charged my mom $50 for taking Brianna, because the whole event was so sugary sweet, it actually made me nauseous.

But Brianna thought the movie was SUPERscary because there was a fairy in it.

She has this irrational fear that the tooth fairy is going to pull out all her teeth to make dentures for old people. I guess you could say she suffers from "fairy phobia."

Anyway, Brianna practically drove me CRAZY, because every time the fairy appeared on the screen, she got really scared, grabbed my arm, and bumped my popcorn. . . .

A TERRIFIED BRIANNA
KEEPS BUMPING MY POPCORN!

I must have dumped my entire box on the nice lady sitting next to me.

But when that nice lady looked like she was going to punch me, I decided it would be safer to eat candy instead.

I was TOO happy when that stupid movie was finally over.

Brianna and I were waiting near the main entrance for Mom to pick us up.

However, when I saw Dad pull up in his Maxwell's Bug Extermination van, I got a really bad feeling. Although, that creepy-looking roach bolted to the top of his van gave MOST people a really bad feeling.

BTW, the roach's name is Max (courtesy of Brianna, "because if I had a puppy, I'd name him Max").

I was like,

OH CRUD!

If anyone from my school saw me getting into Dad's van, my life would be over. I scanned the crowd for middle school kids, and luckily, it was still mostly three- to six-year-olds.

"Hi, girls, hop in! Your mom's still shopping. I just got an emergency call, so you get to ride along to keep me company," my dad said, winking.

I was like, "Um . . . thanks, Dad, but I have an awful lot of homework to do. So could you just drop me home first? PLEASE!" I was trying really hard to remain calm.

My dad glanced at his watch and frowned. "Sorry, but I don't have time to swing by the house. This customer is hysterical and has agreed to pay my emergency rates. She's hosting some kind of big shindig later today and says her house is crawling with bugs inside and out. Hundreds of 'em just showed up out of the blue this morning."

"ICK!!" Brianna blurted, scrunching up her nose.

"Sounds like a box elder infestation to me." Dad continued, "Hopefully, she's not throwing that baby shower your mom is supposed to be attending later today."

I grumpily climbed into the front seat of the van and tried to slouch down really low so no one could see me.

Whenever we stopped at a red light, a bunch of people would point, stare, and laugh. Not at me, at our roach.

For some reason, Brianna thought all the gawkers were just being friendly. So she started smiling, waving, and throwing kisses out the window like she had just been crowned Miss America or something.

And Dad was pretty used to all the rude stares. He just ignored them and hummed along to his *Saturday Night Fever* CD.

Thank goodness I noticed an empty grocery bag sticking out from under the seat.

Even though it said WARNING: TO AVOID SERIOUS INJURY OR DEATH, PLEASE KEEP PLASTIC AWAY FROM VERY YOUNG CHILDREN! I poked two eyeholes in it and pulled it down over my head.

First of all, I WASN'T a very young child.

And second of all, I'd rather live through my WORST nightmare than be spotted riding around in the "roachmobile"!

I have to admit, we were a . . .

FREAK SHOW ON WHEELS!

OMG! It was SO embarrassing!

I wondered how serious my injuries would be if I jumped from a moving vehicle traveling forty-five miles per hour. Assuming I survived, I could at least walk home and end the humiliating ride in Dad's van.

About ten minutes later, we drove up a long driveway that led to a huge house. Wow! Nice house, I thought. Too bad it has bugs!

Brianna stared at the house in awe. "Daddy, can I go inside with you? Pretty please!"

"Sorry, pumpkin, but you'll have to wait out here in the van with your sister and make sure no one steals Max, okay?"

Like, WHO in their right mind would want MAX?!

Two shiny black bugs about a half inch long landed on the window of our van.

"Yep! Box elders, all right," Dad said, eyeing them carefully. "Basically just a harmless eyesore. To spray the entire premises will probably take about thirty minutes. But I'll try to get it done as fast as I can. If you girls need anything, I'll be right inside." Dad unloaded his equipment and lugged it up the front steps. Before he could ring the doorbell, a frantic-looking middle-aged lady in designer clothing opened the door and ushered him in.

Brianna started to pout. "I wanna go in there with DAD!"

"NO! You're supposed to stay here. And watch Max! Remember?" I said sternly.

Brianna wrinkled her nose at me. "YOU watch Max! I gotta go to the bathroom!"

"Brianna, Dad will be back real soon. Can't you just hold it a little longer?"

"NO! I gotta go NOOOWW!"

I was like, Just great! All of this drama for a measly $10.

"Okay, fine," I said, finally giving in. "When we go inside, don't touch anything. Just use the bathroom and come right out, got that?"

"I wanna say hi to Dad too!"

"No! You're gonna use the bathroom, and then we're coming back to the van to wait for . . ."

Before I could finish my sentence, Brianna slid open the van door and dashed to the front steps. By the time I caught up with her, she was already leaning on the doorbell. *Ding-dong! Ding-dong! Ding-dong!*

The flustered-looking lady answered the door again and looked surprised to see Brianna and me.

"Um . . . I really apologize for disturbing you," I stammered. "But we were out in the van waiting for our dad. And my little sister—"

That's when Brianna very rudely interrupted me. . . .

BRIANNA, TOTALLY EMBARRASSING ME

Then she started squirming and making ugly faces for maximum dramatic effect.

My sister was acting like she had the manners of a barnyard animal!

The lady looked at Brianna, then at me, and then back at Brianna. Finally, she stretched her thin red lips into a strained smile.

"Oh! So your dad is our . . . exterminator. Sure, honey, the bathroom is right this way. Follow me."

The inside of the house looked like something out of one of my mom's fancy home and garden magazines.

We were headed down a hallway off the foyer when the lady stopped in her tracks.

"Oh, wait! There's bug spray in all the bathrooms on the main floor. You're going to have to use one upstairs. All of the bedrooms have an attached bathroom. I'd escort you myself, but my caterer is supposed to call me any second now for a final head count."

The telephone rang, and the lady gasped and rushed off, leaving us standing there.

Brianna smiled and darted up the huge staircase ahead of me.

As she entered the first bedroom on the right, she squealed with glee, "Ooh! Pretty!"

It was decorated in shades of pink and had a huge plush rug soft enough to sleep on.

The laptop and big-screen TV were to die for.

My entire bedroom could fit into the walk-in closet.

But, personally, it was a little too sugar-n-spice for my taste.

Not that I was jealous or anything.

Like, how juvenile would THAT be?!

ME AND BRIANNA, IN TOTAL AWE OF THE
FABULOUS BEDROOM!!

"Hey! Can I jump up and down on this princessy
bed?!" Brianna asked.

"NO!" I snapped. "Get down!"

It took all my willpower not to snoop. I wondered what school the girl attended and if we could ever be friends. I bet she had a perfect life. Unlike me.

Brianna skipped into the adjoining bathroom and locked the door behind her. "Wow, I'm gonna get a bathroom like this for my birthday!"

Soon I heard the toilet flush. But after three minutes, she still had not come out.

"Brianna, hurry up!!" I shouted through the door.

"Wait, I'm still washing my hands really good with this strawberry soap, and then I'm going to put on some yummy-smelling cupcake body spray."

"Come on. We have to go back to the van now."

"Wait!! I'm almost done!"

Suddenly I heard a sickeningly familiar voice.

"But, MOM! I CAN'T have my party with these horrible BUGS crawling all over! We should have had it at the country club like I wanted. This is totally YOUR fault!"

I almost wet my pants! It was MACKENZIE HOLLISTER! ☹!

I was like, OMG! OMG! OMG! Today was the party I had not been invited to.

It was like a demented nightmare.

I was trapped in MacKenzie's bedroom, my sister was locked in MacKenzie's bathroom, and my dad was exterminating MacKenzie's house.

And if ALL that wasn't awful enough, our van, with a humongous roach on top of it, was parked in MacKenzie's driveway with MY last name plastered across the side of it (the van, not the roach).

I wanted to dig a deep hole in the lush pink room, crawl into it, and DISAPPEAR!

I pounded on the door. . . .

ME, HAVING A MELTDOWN!

"I'M BUSY. GO AWAY!" Brianna yelled.

"You've been in there long enough. Now open the door!"

"Say 'pretty please.'"

"Pretty please."

"Now say 'pretty please with sugar on top.'"

"Okay. Open the door, pretty please with sugar on top," I begged.

"NO!! I'm NOT done yet!" Brianna answered.

"MOM! This party is going to be a DISASTER! My reputation will be ruined! We HAVE to cancel it."

I could hear MacKenzie's shrieks getting louder. She was coming up the stairs!

"Brianna, open the door quick! PLEASE! It's an emergency!" I hissed through the door.

"Wait! I'm putting on the yummy-smelling cupcake body spray now. Um . . . what's the emergency?"

Now MacKenzie was in the hallway.

"Mom, I'm calling Jessica. She'll never believe this is happening to me. . . ."

I had exactly three seconds to convince Brianna to open the bathroom door.

"Brianna! It's the . . .

TOOTH FAIRY!

She's coming, and we have to get out of here!! NOW!!"

The lock on the door clicked, and Brianna whipped open the door.

She looked even more frightened than she had been at the Princess Sugar Plum movie.

"D—did you just say . . .

T—T—TOOTH FAIRY?!"

"Yes! Come on, let's HIDE! Quick!"

Brianna was panicking and starting to whine. "Where is she? I'm scared! I want Daaaaaddy!"

"Let's hide behind the shower curtain. If we're really quiet, she'll never find us."

Brianna shut up instantly, but her eyes were as big as saucers.

I actually felt a little sorry for her.

I flipped off the bathroom light.

Then we dove into the bathtub and huddled behind the shower curtain.

227

BRIANNA AND ME, HIDING OUT IN
THE BATHROOM!

I could hear MacKenzie stomping around her bedroom and screaming into her cell phone.

"Jess, there's no way I can have this party now! Our house is crawling with bugs! What? . . . How am I supposed to know what they are? They're these big black, um . . . roaches or something. Some guy is here spraying, but now the house stinks! It STINKS, Jess! How can I have a party with the house STINKING?!"

"Nikki, I'm a-scared. I want my daaad-dy! NOW!"

"I BEGGED Mom to let me have my party at the country club! Sofia's mom let her have HER party at the country club. But NOOO! Getting my mom to do anything these days is like pulling TEETH!"

WHY did MacKenzie have to say the T word?!

Brianna totally lost it and started climbing out of the bathtub.

"OH NO! Did you hear that? She says she's going to pull out my TEETH! I wanna go hooome!"

"Brianna!! Wait . . . !" I tackled her and held her in a headlock. Finally, she stopped squirming and went limp.

Then the little brat BIT me!! HARD! I let go of her and yelped in pain like a wounded animal.

"YEEOOOOW!"

But I did it inside my head, so no one else heard it but me.

Brianna scrambled out of the tub, opened the bathroom door, and disappeared into MacKenzie's bedroom!

I froze and held my breath. I could not believe this was happening to me.

Then I thought, maybe this is just a nightmare. Like those scary-weird dreams I was having earlier in the week about Chloe and Zoey. If I could just wake up, this would ALL go away.

So I closed my eyes, pinched myself really hard, and tried to wake up.

But when I opened my eyes, I was STILL standing in MacKenzie's bathtub, with Brianna's (now black-and-blue) teeth marks on my arm next to a throbbing red pinch mark.

I SO wished I had NEVER been BORN!

Suddenly, another idea popped into my head. If I turned on MacKenzie's shower and stood under freezing-cold water for an hour, I might die of pneumonia.

But even that could take a few days, and I wanted this horrible situation to be OVER, RIGHT AWAY!

"OMG! Jess, there's a little KID in my room! . . . How would I know? She appeared out of nowhere. I've told Amanda a million times my room is off-limits to her and her BRATTY little friends. Hold on. . . ."

"MOM . . . !! Amanda and her friends are playing in my room again! Would you please do something . . . ?!"

"Okay, Jess, I'm back. If they so much as touch my makeup again, I swear, I'm going to strangle . . ."

"Don't you dare touch me, you, you . . . WICKED tooth fairy!" Brianna screamed at the top of her lungs.

Suddenly I felt really light-headed. I was sure I was about to faint.

"Hold on a minute, Jess. . . ."

"WHO told you I was the tooth fairy? WHAT are you doing in my bedroom? And WHERE is Amanda?!!"

"You can't have my tooths! NEVER!" Brianna shouted bravely.

"MOM!! AMANDA!! Hold on, Jess. I have to get rid of this little kid. Then I'm going to KILL Amanda! Okay, you! Outta my room, right this—"

"STOP! Let go of me! I LOVE my tooths!"

There was a loud thump, and MacKenzie shrieked. . . .

BRIANNA, BATTLING
THE WICKED TOOTH FAIRY!

"MOM! I've just been attacked by a demonic
munchkin! OMG! I think I'm bruised! I can't wear

my new designer flip-flops with a big bruise on my leg!"

"Are you still there, Jess? I can't have my party like this. I've got a bruise the size of a pancake. NO! . . . I didn't get bruised BY a pancake! I said . . . Hold on . . . !"

I could hear MacKenzie hobbling down the stairs like a one-legged pirate. *Click-klunk, click-klunk, click-klunk.*

"*MOM!* Last week Amanda and her friends put gum in my hair and colored with my lipsticks! Now one of them just . . ."

When it sounded like MacKenzie's screeches were coming from a safe distance away, I jumped out of the bathtub, grabbed Brianna, and tossed her over my shoulder like a sack of rotten potatoes.

Without stopping even once, I hauled her down the stairs, through the hall, to the foyer, and out the front door.

I deposited her butt in the backseat of the van and slammed the door.

My dad was in the back, loading up his equipment.

"Oh, there you girls are! Perfect timing. I'm all done."

As Dad started the van and pulled out, I stared at the house, half expecting MacKenzie to come limping out the front door, ranting that Brianna be arrested for creating a bruise that prevented her from wearing her new designer flip-flops at her birthday party. Amazingly, Brianna sat calmly in the backseat and seemed quite pleased with herself.

"Daddy, guess what? I went to use the bathroom, and after I washed my hands with strawberry soap and put on cupcake body spray, I saw the tooth fairy with rollers in her hair talking on a fairy phone, and she said she was going to strangle me and pull out all of my teeth to make dentures for old people. So when she grabbed me, I kicked her and she let go and started screaming for her mommy. Then she flew back to fairyland to go to a stinky party.

She's NOT very nice, that's for sure! I like Santa and the Easter Bunny much better."

Lucky for us, Dad was only half listening to Brianna's rambling. "Really, pumpkin? So is that what your Princess Sugar Plum movie was about?"

At the next stoplight, I noticed a carload of teen boys pointing and laughing. I put my paper bag back over my head and slouched down in the seat.

I was so mad I could SPIT! All of this drama for a measly ten bucks!!

I'm starting to get really excited because the avant-garde art competition is only eight days away!

I decided to enter my watercolor painting that took me two whole summers at art camp to complete.

I spent more than 130 hours on it.

The only complication is that I gave it to my mom and dad last spring for their sixteenth wedding anniversary.

So it's technically not mine anymore.

It was either my painting or spending my entire life savings of $109.21 to buy them dinner at a fancy restaurant.

But I knew the dinner was going to be a total rip-off, because I watch the Food Network.

All of those five-star restaurants serve really gross stuff like frog legs and snails, and then give you a tiny portion on a really big plate with chocolate syrup drizzled over it and a garnish.

And "garnish" is just a fancy name for a plain old piece of parsley.

So, to save money, Brianna and I decided to cook a romantic candlelit dinner for Mom and Dad as an anniversary surprise.

We took a big bucket and a net to the pond at the park and hunted down some fresh frog legs and snails.

It was MY brilliant idea to make it an

all-you-can-eat

buffet, since we were basically getting the food for FREE....

ME, PLAYING
WITH MY FOOD →

LOVE AT
FIRST SIGHT
→ ♡

RUNAWAY
SNAIL
↓

PARSLEY

FRESH
FROG LEGS
↑

FRESH SNAILS
↑

CHEF NIKKI AND HER ASSISTANT
PREPARE A TASTY GOURMET DINNER OF
FROG LEGS AND SNAILS

Trying to prepare a gourmet dinner was definitely a lot harder than I thought it would be.

The frogs kept jumping out of the bowl, and the snails wouldn't stay on the plate.

Unfortunately, none of those shows on the Food Network explained how to control all the critters while you're trying to cook 'em.

And Brianna was no help WHATSOEVER!

She was SUPPOSED to be my assistant, but she kept swiping the frogs and kissing them to see if they'd turn into princes.

I scolded her really good about that because she had NO IDEA where those frogs' lips had been!

Not surprisingly, Brianna threw a big hissy fit when it came time to put the food in the oven.

She said they were her friends and "friends DON'T COOK friends!"

I had to admit, she DID have a good point. So we decided to take Mom and Dad's anniversary dinner back to the pond and let them go. I guess you could say they were really lucky.

"They" meaning the frogs and snails, not Mom and Dad.

Since our dinner plans fell through, and I didn't want to part with my life savings, I stuck a big red Christmas bow on my watercolor painting and used that as a gift instead.

Mom and Dad must have really loved it, because they paid a ton of money to have it professionally matted and put into an expensive antique frame. Then they hung it in our living room, right over the couch.

Even though it's now a priceless family heirloom with tremendous sentimental value, Mom said I could borrow it for the avant-garde art competition as long as I took really good care of it.

I was like, "Mom, don't worry! I'll be SUPERcareful with your painting. I PROMISE!"

Because, honestly! Like, WHAT could happen?!

I couldn't believe that MacKenzie actually came to school on crutches today.

She even stuck little heart stickers on them so that they matched her new designer purse.

Only someone as vain as MacKenzie would try to look CUTE while hobbling around on crutches.

She didn't have a cast on her leg or anything. Just a Hello Kitty Band-Aid below her left knee.

HOW FAKE IS THAT?!!

According to the latest gossip, MacKenzie was taking scuba diving lessons on Saturday from this really cute ninth grader when she "ruptured her shin" while saving him from drowning.

She supposedly did mouth-to-mouth resuscitation on him until the ambulance arrived.

And since the poor guy's dying wish was for her to escort him to the hospital, she was forced to cancel her birthday party.

So she rescheduled it for Saturday, October 12th, at her parents' country club.

I was like, Yeah, RIGHT!

MacKenzie is such a LIAR and a DRAMA QUEEN!

Why couldn't she just tell the truth and admit her party was canceled because her house was infested with bugs and stank from bug spray?

Anyway, today I could hardly wait for lunch.

Chloe and Zoey were even more excited than I was. We sat at our usual table and snarfed down our lunch as fast as we could.

Then I rolled up Zoey's sleeve, took out my lucky pen, and got started on her tattoo.

She kept giggling and squirming and complaining that it tickled.

So I said . . .

"LISTEN, ZOEY, SHUT UP AND SIT STILL OR I'M GONNA TURN ANY STRAY INK MARKS INTO UGLY BABY SNAKES!!"

Lucky for her, she stopped moving after that.

Practically everyone in the cafeteria was staring at us, but I ignored them and kept right on working. Zoey's tattoo turned out really cool, and she loved it. . . .

READING...
AN EXTREME SPORT!

I was just getting started on Chloe's tattoo when the weirdest thing happened.

Jason Feldman got up, left the CCP table, and sat down at OUR table to watch. He's just THE most popular guy in the entire school and president of student council.

On the "Cuteness Scale," I would say he is a 9.93 out of 10.

"You're doing a tattoo with a pen?! Cool! It looks so real. I should know because my brother just got one for his eighteenth birthday."

"It's our special LSA project for National Library Week," Chloe explained, and batted her eyelashes at him all flirtylike.

"Yeah! And all the latest fashion magazines say tattoos are HAWT!" Zoey added, and plastered a big fat cheesy smile on her face.

Those two were acting so phony-baloney, it was sickening. I thought I was going to puke up my lunch right in Jason's lap.

"So what do I have to do to get one?" Jason asked excitedly. "Donate a book or something? Do you have a sign-up sheet?"

Chloe's and Zoey's faces lit up at the same time, and I could see the little lightbulbs click on in their brains.

I just sighed and rolled my eyes. First it was the tattoo thing, then *Ballet of the Zombies*, and then running away to live in the secret underground tunnels at the NYC public library.

I didn't know if I could put up with much more of this drama.

Chloe fluttered her eyelashes at Jason again. "Well, Nikki is art director, I'm overseeing book procurement, and Zoey here handles scheduling. Zoey, would you please give Jason our sign-up sheet?"

"Um . . . what sign-up sheet?" Zoey asked, looking confused.

Chloe winked at her and said really loudly, "You know, the *SIGN-UP SHEET* in your *NOTEBOOK*, silly!"

Finally, Zoey caught on. "Oh, THAT sign-up sheet! Of course!" She gazed at Jason and giggled nervously.

Zoey whipped out her notebook, tore out a sheet of paper, scribbled TATTOO SIGN-UP SHEET across the top, and handed it to Chloe.

Chloe added the words BOOK DONATION REQUIRED (NEW OR USED)!! in big bold letters and gave it to Jason.

I was shocked and appalled to see Chloe and Zoey lying like that. I always felt honesty was a very important quality in a friend.

Jason wrote his name on the sign-up sheet and then yelled to his lunch table on the other side of the cafeteria, "Hey, Crenshaw! Get Thompson and come check this out."

Ryan Crenshaw is a 9.86, and Matt Thompson is a 9.98. They both came over and sat down at OUR table, right next to Jason. Then the three of them started laughing and talking to me, Chloe, and Zoey like we were CCP girls or something.

That's when I decided that, although an honest friend is nice, an "I-can-hook-you-up-with-really-cute-guys" friend is far better.

And besides, Chloe and Zoey weren't actually lying. They were just over-embellishing some fabricated truths.

Even though I was enjoying all of the unexpected attention, there was an incessant gnawing deep down inside my gut that had me really worried.

WHY were the three most popular CCP guys suddenly sitting at a lunch table, flirting with Chloe, Zoey, and me, the three biggest DORKS in the school?

And WHAT exactly did they want from us?

Then I had to force myself to ponder the most INTRIGUING and TROUBLING question of all. . . .

Was my lucky pen going to MELT from all of the CCP GUY HOTNESS?!

Here are the THREE reasons why I was a little worried about my pen. . . .

JASON
(The Prep)

RYAN
(The Jock)

MATT
(The Bad Boy)

Within minutes, seven more guys had crashed our table and were passing around the sign-up sheet and boasting about how wicked their tat was going to be.

I finally finished up Chloe's tattoo, and she said it was perfect. . . .

CHLOE'S TATTOO

Jason rolled up his sleeve and took Chloe's place. "Hey, listen up! Mine is gonna say 'GAMER-4-LIFE'!!"

All of the guys started slapping him on the back and giving him high fives and fist bumps. He was acting all smug, like he was getting a new sports car or something.

Then a large crowd of girls gathered around the large crowd of guys to watch me work on Jason's tattoo.

"Isn't she the new girl?"

"I think her locker is right next to MacKenzie's."

"She's, like, THE best artist in the entire school."

"Hey, I wanna sign up! Give me the sheet next. . . ."

"What's her name?"

"Mikki, Rikki, or Vicki, I think."

"Whatever her name is, the girl's got SKILLZ."

"I'm SOOO jealous! I can't draw a stick figure."

"She's in my French class. Her name is Nikki Maxwell!"

"I'd LOVE to draw on Jason Feldman. He's HAWT!"

"OMG! I'd give ANYTHING to be Nikki Maxwell!"

MY HUGE CROWD OF ADMIRING FANS

I was starting to feel like a POP STAR!

The only CCPs not at our table were MacKenzie and her little group. They were GLARING at us from across the cafeteria.

By the end of lunch period, I had completed seven tattoos, Chloe had collected nine books, and Zoey had scheduled eleven people to get tattoos tomorrow at lunch.

We decided to call our new LSA project:

"Ink Exchange: Trade a Book for a Tattoo!"

By the end of the day, the ENTIRE school was buzzing about us.

Mrs. Peach said collecting books for charity was a wonderful idea, and she was really proud of us.

Brandon even congratulated me and said he wanted to interview me for the school newspaper on Friday since I was "breaking news."

He said he planned to photograph students showing off their new tattoos for the article.

Now I can hardly wait for Friday to get here ☺! There's a chance we might actually become good friends.

But the absolute, most mind-blowing thing about all of this is that Chloe, Zoey, and I started the school day as LSA DORKS and ended it as CCP DIVAS!

HOW COOL IS THAT?!
☺!!

TUESDAY, OCTOBER 1

	Today	Total
TATTOOS	17	24
BOOKS	34	43

This tattoo craze has really caught on at WCD!

I did eleven more during lunch, and most of the CCPs sat at our table to watch.

Chloe, Zoey, and I thought it was pretty cool hanging out with them, and they were not mean or snotty like we thought they'd be.

I guess it was just a matter of getting to know them better.

Surprisingly, I ended up doing another six tattoos while I was on LSA duty. It seemed like everyone and their mother was getting library passes during fifth-hour homeroom and pestering me.

But Mrs. Peach said she didn't mind me not shelving books, since I was working on our group project.

So far, we've collected a total of forty-three books for charity, which is fantastic.

But it was mainly because Chloe decided to start charging two books for a tattoo instead of one.

Zoey and I thought one book was perfectly fine, and we told her so.

But Chloe said that, since she was the director of book procurement, it was HER decision, not ours, so it didn't matter what we thought.

Now, how RUDE was THAT?!

I was like,

"Okay, Chloe! We're SUPPOSED to be doing this as a group project! Who made you QUEEN?!" . . .

CHLOE THE GREAT, QUEEN OF BOOKS

But I just said it in my head, so no one else heard it but me.

So now we're getting TWO books for each tattoo, although it seems a bit GREEDY, if you ask me. ☹!

WEDNESDAY, OCTOBER 2

	Today	Total
TATTOOS	19	43
BOOKS	57	100

I used to daydream about everyone at WCD knowing my name.

And today my dream finally came true!

More than two dozen people said hi to me before I even got to my first-hour class.

It made me happy to have so many new friends ☺.

In biology, we had to choose a lab partner and look at dust mites under a microscope.

I thought for sure that Brandon was going to ask me to work with him. But three people interrupted him while he was trying to talk to me.

They were all like, "Hey, Nikki, let's work together so we can talk about my new tattoo design."

But I didn't want to talk to people I hardly knew about tattoos.

I wanted to have a really deep emo convo with Brandon about dust mites.

In the end, I got stuck with Alexis Hamilton, the captain of the cheerleaders.

The whole time we were working, all she did was blab about how they (the cheerleaders) needed me to come up with a "superhot" tattoo for their big game against Central, which, BTW, is on Friday.

But I already knew this because I overheard them talking about it in front of my locker this morning.

A few of them were waiting around for me after second hour, and they seemed pretty cranky.

It wasn't like I was afraid of them or anything;

I just jumped inside my locker because I can be a little shy at times. . . .

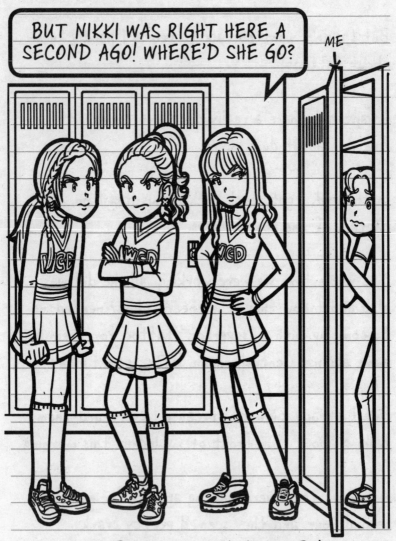

ME, BEING HUNTED DOWN BY
AN ANGRY MOB OF CHEERLEADERS!

Anyway, I told Alexis that everyone had to sign up with Zoey first.

But she said Zoey had a waiting list of 149 people through next Wednesday, and she needed the tats right away since it was kind of an emergency.

Alexis said she had already donated three books for each tattoo to Chloe, and Chloe was authorizing the squad to be placed at the top of the waiting list.

So NOW it was THREE BOOKS?!

I told Alexis that since Zoey was director of scheduling and Chloe was director of book procurement, she should probably just ignore Chloe.

Then Alexis got an attitude about the whole thing and refused to talk to me or help write our lab report on dust mites.

Talk about a CRUDDY lab partner ☹!

But what really upset me was that Zoey had scheduled 149 people without asking me first. I have a French test on Friday and a geometry test next Monday, and I'm barely pulling a B in each of those classes.

How am I supposed to study if I'm staying up past midnight EVERY night designing tats for all of these people?! And I haven't had time to eat lunch for the past two days!

Then, as I was leaving class, Samantha Gates stopped me to say how much she loved her tat of her favorite boy band. She said all of her friends in the drama club wanted one too.

Samantha invited me to hang out with them after school on Friday, and I told her I'd let her know.

But how can I have a social life when I have to draw tattoos 24/7?

!

	Today	Total
TATTOOS	33	76
BOOKS	99	199

I had a really **CRUDDY** day today!

It seems that all Chloe, Zoey, and everyone cares about is TATTOOS. I came to school early and did nine.

Then I did fourteen at lunchtime and another ten during library. That's thirty-three tattoos!

Then I overheard Zoey tell Chloe, behind my back, that I worked "slower than a constipated snail in an ice storm" and I needed to speed up since she now had 216 people on the waiting list for next week. I was so NOT doing 216 tattoos in one week!

And I told Zoey that right to her face ☹.

In a really friendly way ☺.

Then Chloe wanted to know why I told Alexis to ignore her.

She said that, since the cheerleaders had a big game, she thought they should be put at the top of the list for tomorrow.

That's when Zoey said that, as the director of scheduling, the decision was HERS alone and she didn't care WHAT Chloe thought.

Which was the EXACT same thing Chloe had said to us a few days ago.

Then Mrs. Peach came over and asked us to PLEASE lower our voices because we were, after all, in a library.

But I knew better.

It WASN'T a library!

It was SUPPOSED to be a library, but it was ACTUALLY a . . .

ME

HORRIBLE, WICKED TATTOO SWEATSHOP ☹!

FRIDAY, OCTOBER 4

TATTOOS TODAY—A BIG FAT ZERO!

BOOKS TODAY—A BIG FAT ZERO!

WHY?

First of all, Chloe and Zoey were mad because I didn't come to school early, and they had seventeen people waiting for tattoos.

Well, EXCUUUUSE me! But I had a French test today that I had to study for.

Then, at lunch, there were twenty-five people waiting. But instead of sitting at table 9 and helping me, Chloe and Zoey sat at the CCP table on the other side of the cafeteria.

I could see them giggling and acting all flirty with Jason, Ryan, and Matt while I was supposed to be working my butt off like CINDERELLA or somebody!

But I nearly FREAKED when I saw MacKenzie give Chloe and Zoey INVITATIONS to her rescheduled party for next Saturday!

They were pink envelopes with big white satin ribbons tied around them, just like the one she had given ME.

And then taken back when she UNINVITED me!

Chloe and Zoey were acting all happy and sucking up to MacKenzie, even though they knew she HATED my guts.

SO I did the most mature and rational thing possible under the circumstances. . . .

I QUIT 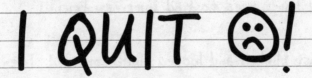!

If I have to draw one more tattoo, I'm going to

VOMIT!

I thought Chloe and Zoey were my real friends.

But now I can see that they were just USING me all along to earn that trip to NYC for National Library Week.

HOW COULD THEY DO THIS TO ME?!

Then Brandon came up to my locker all smiley and said he wanted to interview me for the newspaper during library.

But I told him to just forget it because my tattoo career was OVER!

He asked me if I was okay, and I said, "Yeah, it's all good! I just need to find some new friends."

He just blinked and looked kinda confused. Then he shrugged and walked away.

So now it's like CHLOE, ZOEY, and BRANDON are all TRIPPIN'.

I hope the three of them have a blast at MacKenzie's little party, since they all got invited and

I DIDN'T!!

But it wasn't like I was jealous of them or anything.

I mean, how totally juvenile would THAT be?!

☹!!

I had the most horrible nightmare! The scariest thing was that it felt SO real.

IT WAS LIKE EVERYONE WAS OUT TO GET ME!! . . .

MY HORRIBLE NIGHTMARE!!

I was in my pj's, trying to put away a huge stack of library books.

MacKenzie was laughing at me and spitting bugs on me!

Chloe and Zoey were flying on a huge ink pen, trying to capture me in a net!

And a giant camera bug was trying to take my photo for the school newspaper!

But all I could hear was the fifth-hour bell ringing and ringing.

Thank goodness I finally woke up.

That's when I realized it was morning and the telephone was ringing, not the fifth-hour bell.

I dragged myself out of bed and answered the phone on my desk.

It was my grandma calling to tell us she was planning

to come visit us for two weeks at the end of November.

I told her my parents must already be out running errands or something since they hadn't answered the phone.

Then she asked me how I was doing, and I told her not so good.

I said I was thinking about transferring out of my school and asked her what she would do if she were me.

She said it was NOT so much about the school I chose, but whether I chose to be a chicken or a champion.

Which, of course, had ABSOLUTELY NOTHING to do with ANYTHING! Since Grandma was talking out of her head again, I told her that I loved her but that I had to go because someone was at the door. Then I hung up.

I wasn't lying to her, because, unfortunately, Brianna and Miss Penelope were at my bedroom door.

Miss Penelope wanted me to watch her and Brianna do a medley of songs from Princess Sugar Plum's greatest hits album complete with dance choreography.

Okay, that's when my brain almost

EXPLODED.

I had been awake for less than three minutes and had already been forced to deal with my senile grandma, my hyperactive sister, and a wacky puppet.

I climbed back into bed, pulled the covers up over my head, and SCREAMED for two whole minutes.

So many FREAKS and not enough CIRCUSES!!

!!

PLEASE, PLEASE, PLEASE make all of this NOT be really happening to me.

Today has been the WORST day of my ENTIRE life ☹!!

It all started Sunday night when I was sitting at my desk doing review problems for my geometry test.

If I did really well on it, I'd be able to raise my grade up to a solid B.

My mom came into my room around midnight to tell me she was leaving the house extra early in the morning to chaperone a field trip for Brianna's class.

"Nikki, since you have a test and the art competition tomorrow, it's REALLY important that you set your alarm clock so you don't oversleep in the morning."

I was like, "Thanks, Mom. Good night!"

I really DID plan to set my clock. As soon as I finished my geometry problems.

But the next thing I knew, it was morning. And I was STILL sitting at my desk with my geometry book open.

I just about had a heart attack because, according to my clock, it was 7:36 a.m. on MONDAY, and my first-hour class started at 8:00 a.m.!

The only logical explanation was that I must have

FALLEN ASLEEP

while studying at my desk. . . .

ME, SNOOZING (AND DROOLING ALL OVER
MY GEOMETRY BOOK)!

My day was off to a very bad start!

I had overslept, I didn't have a ride to school, my
painting needed to be turned in for the art show,

and my geometry test started in less than twenty-four, no, make that twenty-three, minutes.

Even the weather perfectly matched my miserable mood. It was dark, overcast, and pouring rain.

I was fighting back my tears when suddenly I heard the low rumble of our garage door opening. I ran to my bedroom window and spotted the flicker of bright headlights.

IT WAS MY DAD ☺! And he was leaving the house.

I rushed around my room in a panic, trying to get dressed before he pulled out. I jumped into my jeans and slid on my jacket. When I couldn't find one of my shoes, I decided to just change into my PE shoes once I got to school.

I grabbed my backpack and my painting and dashed downstairs like a maniac. By the time I got out the front door, my dad was already pulling into the street.

I ran down our driveway, waving my arms and
screaming hysterically. . . .

ME, CHASING AFTER THE VAN

Only, I couldn't run very fast because I was loaded down with my backpack and the painting. Of course, my bunny slippers didn't help the situation either.

Unfortunately, my dad DIDN'T see me ☹!

So I just stood there in our driveway in the pouring rain, feeling really, really cruddy.

I couldn't believe I was going to miss the art show, receive an F on my geometry test, and get an unexcused absence, all in the same day. I got this large, painful lump in my throat, and I felt like crying again.

But my dad must have finally noticed me in his rearview mirror or something, because suddenly he slammed on his brakes.

SKKKRREEEEEECCHH!!

I took off running down the street toward the van as fast as I could.

As I climbed in, Dad chuckled. "Does Sleeping Beauty need a ride to school, or are you waiting for your prince?!"

I ignored his corny little joke and collapsed into the backseat of the van. I was soaking wet, but I felt happy and relieved.

All was not lost! Yet, anyway.

But I also felt really anxious. For the first time this year, I was riding to school in the roachmobile!!

And if anyone saw me getting out of it, I was going to absolutely DIE!

By the time we pulled up to the front of the school, the rain had finally stopped.

Thank goodness the only other vehicle around was a small truck with some men in uniform carrying in large flat panels.

I guessed that they were the displays for the art show.

I thanked Dad for the ride, grabbed my painting, and climbed out of the van.

Just as I was about to slam the door shut, he waved and pointed to my backpack on the floor.

"Hey, I think you're forgetting something!"

I carefully set my painting on the ground and leaned it against the side of the van. Then I climbed back in and grabbed my backpack.

"I think I'm all set now! Thanks again, Dad!"

I waved and then slammed the van door shut.

I could NOT believe that I had actually made it to school in one piece with six minutes to spare. And not a single soul had spotted me getting out of the roachmobile, which was a miracle in and of itself.

Then I noticed a girl wearing matching designer raincoat, hat, and boots climbing out of the back of the truck parked in front of us.

"Hey, careful with that, buddy! It's a piece of art, not a piece of plywood!" she snarled at one of the men.

I froze and thought about trying to duck back into the van to hide until she left. But it was too late!

MacKenzie's mouth dropped open.

At first she had a look of shock on her face as she stared at me, my van, and Max (yes, the roach). Then her lips spread into a really evil grin.

"Wait a minute! YOU'RE the same Maxwell as Maxwell's Bug Extermination?! And what is that hideous brown thing on top of your van, a dead moose?! Let me guess, it's supposed to be a matching set with those two dead bunnies on your feet?!"

I just glared at her and didn't say a word.

Okay, MacKenzie was the undisputed winner if we were competing for richest snob, cutest designer wardrobe, most friends, coolest bedroom, or biggest house.

But we WEREN'T.

Avant-garde art was all about pure, unadulterated TALENT, which MacKenzie could NOT buy with her parents' money.

It was her Fab-4-Ever fashion illustrations against my watercolor—

That's when I suddenly remembered.

OMG!! MY PAINTING!

I spun around and lunged to grab it just as my dad was pulling out.

But I was too late! . . .

I gasped and watched in horror as the van tire slowly crushed glass, antique wood frame, my hopes, and my dreams. . . .

THE VAN RUNS OVER MY PAINTING!

It was shockingly painful to see the unique expression of me that had taken more than 130 hours to capture in watercolor so brutally destroyed in a matter of seconds.

But the torn, twisted, and splintered mess on the side of the curb was not nearly as ugly as MacKenzie's final insult.

"Oh no! Was that your little art project?! Too bad! Hey, just throw some bugs on it and enter it as a modern art piece called *Maxwell's Bugs on Garbage*."

Then she cackled like a witch and sashayed off.

I just **HATE** it when MacKenzie sashays!

I watched sadly as the roachmobile turned the corner and disappeared down the road.

For the first time in my life, I wished I were inside it, warm and dry and speeding away.

Away from MacKenzie.

Away from friends who were really NOT my friends.

Away from Westchester Country Day Middle School.

I didn't fit in at this place, and I was sick and tired of trying.

I sat down on the side of the curb, next to the pieces of my painting, and cried.

The rain started to pour again, but I didn't care.

I had been sitting there, like, forever, trying to sort things out inside my head, when I noticed it had stopped raining. On ME, anyway.

Then I recognized that faint aroma of Snuggle fabric softener, Axe body spray, and red licorice.

I looked up and was surprised and slightly embarrassed to see Brandon standing there, holding an umbrella over me. . . .

BRANDON AND ME IN THE RAIN

"Are you okay?"

I didn't answer.

Then he extended his hand. I just looked at it and sighed.

If I sat out on the curb in the rain much longer, I'd probably catch a really bad cold and end up missing several days of school.

Which, under the circumstances, didn't sound like such a bad thing.

I grabbed ahold of Brandon's hand, and he slowly pulled me up off the wet curb.

I could NOT believe we were doing this stupid little scene all over again. How PATHETIC!

I rolled my eyes, sniffed, and wiped my runny nose on the back of my hand.

I was NOT going to let him see me cry.

Both of us just stood there not saying anything. He was staring at me and I was staring at the ground.

Suddenly, Brandon dug deep into his pocket and fished out a wrinkled-looking piece of tissue.

"Um . . . I think you have . . . something on your face?"

"Probably SNOT!" I muttered sarcastically, and snatched the tissue from his hand.

"Yeah. Probably," he said, trying hard not to smile. "Like . . . I dig those shoes!"

"They're NOT shoes. They're bunny slippers! I was in a REALLY big hurry this morning, okay?!"

I blew my nose at him loudly and angrily.
HOOONKK!

"So . . . um, it looks like you had a little accident with your art project."

"I wouldn't call it 'little.'"

"Well, if it will make you feel any better, MacKenzie is entering some life-size paper dolls. I'd say your painting is STILL better than hers. Even in twenty-seven pieces. With mud smeared on it. And a few worms."

A mischievous grin slowly spread across Brandon's face.

"Come on. Everyone knows you have more talent in your smallest burp than—"

"Yeah! I know. I KNOW . . . !" I said, interrupting him and blushing uncontrollably.

I HATE it when he does that to me!

Okay, even though I was mad at the world, I had to admit, this whole thing WAS a little funny. In a really bent sort of way.

Finally, I smiled at Brandon, and he winked at me.

He is such a DORK!

But in a good way.

He has a slightly weird sense of humor and is friendly and a little shy ALL at the same time.

And, unlike me, he doesn't obsess about what other people think about him.

I think THAT is probably the coolest thing about him.

"Thanks for the umbrella!"

"Hey, no prob!"

Then we both walked to the front entrance.

Even though the building was warm, I felt really chilled.

My slippers were soaked, and it seemed like I was wearing sponges dipped in ice water on my feet.

"I need to get my shoes out of my locker and then go to the office to call my dad. Hopefully, he can drop off some dry clothing."

"So . . . I'll walk you to the office, if you don't mind. My class is on the way."

As Brandon and I made our way down the hall, some people stopped and stared, while others pointed and laughed. But I just ignored them.

I knew I looked pretty crazy. With every step I took, my bunny slippers went *sloshie-squeak, sloshie-squeak, sloshie-sqeak,* and left small puddles of water behind me.

When I finally got to my locker, there was a large crowd of kids gathered around it.

At first I thought they were there for tattoos, but everyone quickly scattered.

Then I saw what they were looking at. . . .

SOMEONE HAD VANDALIZED MY LOCKER!!

It felt like I had been punched in my stomach so hard, I could hardly breathe.

I covered my mouth and tried to blink back my tears for what seemed like the tenth time this morning.

Someone had written on my locker in what appeared to be Ravishing Red-Hot Cinnamon Twist lip gloss. Which, BTW, was MacKenzie's favorite.

"I—I'm really sorry!" Brandon stammered. "Only a real loser would do something as mean and stupid as . . ."

But I didn't hear the rest of what he said. I turned around, pushed my way through the crowded hallway, and went straight to the office to call my parents.

I couldn't take it anymore! I was leaving Westchester Country Day Middle School. And NEVER coming back!

☹!!

Today I stayed home from school with a cold and just lounged in bed all day and drank lemon tea.

After my dad picked me up from school yesterday, I started thinking that maybe I had overreacted.

Watching my painting being smashed into a zillion pieces had been pretty traumatic, but it was mainly MacKenzie who was making my life miserable.

Maybe WCD wasn't such a horrible place. Maybe if I tried talking to Chloe and Zoey, we could go back to being friends again. Maybe Brandon hadn't written me off as a total loser.

So yesterday I called the library desk during fifth hour to talk to Chloe and Zoey. Plus, I was a teensy bit curious about how MacKenzie's art project had turned out. Okay, I admit, I was DYING to know!

"Library front desk, Zoey speaking."

"Hi, Zoey, it's me, Nikki. I was just calling to see how you guys are doing. You'll NEVER believe what happened to me this morning."

Then I heard Chloe's muffled voice in the background.

"OMG! It's her?! Just say you can't talk right now because we're really busy. We don't have time to waste."

"Um . . . what's up, Nikki? Brandon told us everything that happened. Actually, he's here right now. Too bad about your art project . . . ," Zoey stammered nervously.

"Yeah, I know. So, what are the three of you do—"

"Listen, Nikki, I really have to hang up now. We're really busy with, um . . . a project. Chloe and Brandon said hi."

"Wait, Zoey! I just wanted to—"

"Sorry, gotta go. See you tomorrow. Bye."

CLICK!

After that conversation, there was no doubt in my mind that Chloe, Zoey, and Brandon practically hated me.

So there wasn't really anything left to do but make plans to transfer to a new school.

And have a really good CRY!! . . .

Which is what I've been doing on and off for the past twenty-four hours.

The only good thing that's come out of all of this is that my parents have been so worried about my emotional state, they've finally agreed to let me transfer to the nearby public school.

I thanked my dad for arranging the scholarship and all, but I told him it just hadn't worked out.

Surprisingly, Mom and Dad also took the news about their anniversary painting being destroyed really well.

I even promised I would paint them a new one, although Brianna insisted that she wanted to do it instead.

"Don't worry, Mom and Dad! I'm almost done making you a brand-new anniversary present, and it's way better than Nikki's dumb ol' painting!"

But I had a really bad feeling about Brianna's art project.

When I asked her if she had used finger paints or crayons, she said, "Nope! A black permanent marker. And I drew it over the couch in the exact same spot where your painting was hanging!"

Brianna said her drawing was called . . .

THE MAXWELL FAMILY VISITS PRINCESS SUGAR PLUM ON BABY UNICORN ISLAND

When Mom saw Brianna's wall mural, she just about fainted.

And then Brianna tried to get out of it by blaming Miss Penelope.

It was kind of nice to laugh again after feeling so hopelessly depressed.

☺!!

My parents and I drove over to WCD forty-five minutes early so we could get everything taken care of before the students started arriving.

As Mom and Dad sat in the office chatting with the secretary and completing the school-transfer paperwork, I couldn't help noticing the colorful displays off the main entryway for the art competition.

No matter how much I tried to convince myself I didn't care, I just HAD to know if MacKenzie had won.

It was like I was obsessed or something.

If I hurried, I could stop by the art competition for a few minutes and still have time to clean out my locker, get back to the office, and be out of the building before anyone spotted me.

"Well, I better get going," I muttered to my parents.

I grabbed the empty cardboard box I had brought to carry the junk from my locker and headed down the hall.

The art exhibit was set up in the large student lounge near the cafeteria and was divided by grades.

I hurried past the sixth- and seventh-grade displays to the eighth-grade section.

There were about twenty-four entries, and I immediately noticed MacKenzie's.

Like everything she did, it was big, bold, and over the top.

She had painted seven life-size mannequins dressed in her Fab-4-Ever fashions on six-foot-tall panels.

I had to admit, she was actually a pretty good fashion illustrator.

But the strange thing was that I didn't see her first-place award.

Although, knowing MacKenzie, she probably had already taken it home so her parents could have it bronzed to match her baby shoes.

Then again, maybe NOT.

I was surprised to see the blue ribbon was hanging on the very last display.

I couldn't help pitying the poor artist who would have to put up with the drama over MacKenzie's very public and humiliating defeat.

The winning display was a series of sixteen 8 x 10 close-up black-and-white photographs of inked artwork.

When I read the title and the artist's name, I totally

FREAKED OUT!...

IT WAS MY TATTOO ARTWORK!!

I immediately recognized my drawings on Zoey's

shoulder, Chloe's arm, Tyler's neck, Sophia's ankle, Matt's wrist, and on and on.

So THIS must have been the "project" Chloe, Zoey, and Brandon were working on when they said they were too busy to talk to me on the telephone Monday afternoon.

Slowly but surely, the reality of the situation started to sink in.

I was like, "OMG! I WON first place in AVANT-GARDE ART! FIRST PLACE and SEVEN HUNDRED FIFTY DOLLARS!"

Thanks to Chloe, Zoey, and Brandon! They must have cooked up this elaborate scheme after my painting got destroyed.

And that AWESOME display with MY name on it had probably taken hours to complete.

I was SO wrong about them.

They were the BEST friends EVER!

And more than a dozen other kids had volunteered to be photographed.

All of this totally BLEW MY MIND!

Maybe WCD was not such a horrible place after all. I actually had real friends here.

And, of course, it didn't hurt that I was now rich, rich, rich beyond my wildest dreams!

I hurried back to the office in a daze and burst inside.

"Mom, Dad! I've changed my mind. I want to stay!"

They both looked surprised.

"Honey, are you okay?" my mom asked, concerned.

"Actually, Mom, I'm GREAT! I've changed my mind. I want to stay. PLEASE!"

"Well, it's up to you. Are you sure?" my dad said, putting down his pen.

"I'm sure. I'm REALLY sure!"

The secretary gathered the papers from my dad, ripped them in half, and tossed them into the wastebasket.

"This is great news!" She beamed. "And congratulations on your first place in the art show! You're coming to the reception for the winners this Saturday, right? They'll be giving out the cash awards, and the catered dinner is fabulous."

My parents looked totally confused. "I thought you said you didn't enter the art—" my mom began, but I quickly interrupted her.

"Listen, I'll explain all of this later. Like, don't you both have somewhere to be?" I smiled and waved good-bye to them, hoping they would take the hint and get lost.

Mom kissed my forehead. "Okay, hon! We're glad you've decided to hang in there."

"Yeah, and you can thank Maxwell's Extermination for hooking you up!" my dad said, and winked. "I knew it would work out for you here, if you just gave it a chance."

"Well, I gotta go! Oh. Here, Dad!" I tossed him the cardboard box. "Can you get rid of this for me?"

I turned and rushed out of the office. Students were starting to fill up the halls, and a few actually congratulated me.

As I made my way back to my locker, I wasn't quite sure what to expect, but I was ready and willing to deal with it.

The graffiti had been cleaned up, thank goodness.

But there was something new on my locker. . . .

Nikki,
Please meet us in
the janitor's closet
ASAP!
It's <u>very</u>,<u>very</u>
important!

Chloe and Zoey

I knocked on the door of the janitor's closet and then peeked inside.

Chloe and Zoey were sitting on the floor in a corner and looking pretty sad.

I felt kind of sorry for them.

"Nikki, we owe you an apology for the way we acted," Chloe said. "We got really carried away with all of the tattoo and book stuff. And that wasn't fair to you."

"Yeah! And we learned who our real friends are too. The CCPs wanted to hang out with us as long as YOU were doing the tattoos. What a bunch of phonies!" Zoey complained.

"Actually, I kind of figured that out too. That angry mob of cheerleaders was too scary!" I said, shuddering at the memory.

"Listen, please don't be mad, Nikki!" Chloe said, starting to tear up. "But we have a confession to make. We kind of did something behind your back."

Zoey cleared her throat. "Well, after we heard about the accident with your painting, we rounded up the kids with your best tattoo artwork, and Brandon took pictures of them during lunch. Then he printed out the photographs on the computer in the newspaper office. Mrs. Peach let the three of us work on your entry the entire afternoon in the library. We called it *The Student Body*."

"And you'll never guess what happened," Chloe sniffed, blinking back tears.

"I WON!"

"YOU WON!!" they said together.

"Wait! You KNEW?!" Zoey asked, surprised.

"Yeah. I just found out a few minutes ago."

"We know we shouldn't have done it without asking you first. But there wasn't time. You're not mad at us, are you?" Chloe asked, and gave me jazz hands to try to lighten the mood.

"Actually, I am. I'm VERY ANGRY!" I hissed.

Chloe and Zoey both hung their heads and stared at the floor.

"We're sorry, Nikki. We were just trying to help . . . ," Zoey muttered.

"You're supposed to be my friends. How could you two do this to me? I'm so TICKED! I would have given ANYTHING to have seen THE LOOK ON MACKENZIE'S FACE WHEN SHE LOST!" I was trying so hard not to laugh that I was starting to snort.

At first, both girls blinked and looked bewildered. Then, slowly, smiles spread across their faces until they were grinning from ear to ear.

"OMG! Nikki, you should have seen her." Chloe giggled. "When they announced you as the winner, she went into shock!"

"It was hilarious! MacKenzie threw a hissy fit right there in front of the judges!" Zoey snickered.

Pretty soon we were laughing and joking in the janitor's closet, just like old times.

"Uh-oh! I think I just heard the first bell," I groaned.

"Let's get out of here before we start smelling like a mildewy mop!"

Chloe and Zoey opened the door and then stood there waiting for me to leave first.

"Talent before . . . BRAINS!" Zoey winked and then gave me the stink eye.

"Talent before . . . BEAUTY!" Chloe grinned and then gave me jazz hands.

"Hey, girlfriends, I see the talent! But, other than ME, there's definitely no brains or beauty in here!" I teased.

That's when Chloe and Zoey both socked me on my arm. "OW!!" I giggled. "That HURT!!"

!!

There must have been a big sale at the mall yesterday or something, because four girls were wearing the EXACT same outfit. I hadn't really noticed it until I overheard MacKenzie ridiculing them in the hall.

"OMG! Look at that! They're ALL wearing the same butt-ugly ensemble! Wait, don't tell me. They were giving them away for FREE with a purchase of a McDonald's Happy Meal!"

It was only 7:45 a.m., and I was already visualizing DUCT TAPE over her mouth. When MacKenzie finally noticed me, she tried to act all innocent.

"Just in case you're wondering, I DIDN'T write 'Bug Girl' on your locker. Lots of people wear Ravishing Red-Hot Cinnamon Twist, you know."

I just rolled my eyes at her. That girl is SUCH a liar! I didn't believe her for one second.

MacKenzie flipped her hair and gazed at her
perfect image in her mirror. . . .

ME, TOTALLY IGNORING MACKENZIE!

"Besides, even if I did it, you don't have any proof!" Then she applied her morning layer of lip gloss.

Since I was stuck having a locker next to MacKenzie's for the rest of the year, I decided to utilize the mind-over-matter coping strategy that Zoey had developed.

In my MIND, I was so OVER being impressed with MacKenzie, because she didn't MATTER!

Although, I have to admit, those chandelier earrings she was wearing were to die for.

Why is it that huge dangly earrings look really

GLAMTASTIC

on the CCP girls?

But when normal girls (like me) wear them, we end up needing RECONSTRUCTIVE COSMETIC SURGERY. . . .

Anyway, Chloe, Zoey, and I sat together at lunch at table 9, and a lot of people stopped by to ask about tattoos.

Since our Ink Exchange program was such a big hit, and we had already collected almost two hundred books for charity, we decided to continue it for just three days each month, starting in November.

It was going to be great NOT having to hide inside my locker between classes due to my fear of angry mobs—I mean, my shyness.

And now I'm actually starting to look forward to attending National Library Week at the NYC public library.

We have a really good chance of being selected.

I mean, just think about it! Chloe, Zoey, and me in Manhattan for five days without our parents!

How EXCITING would THAT be?!

We'd have Friends, Fun, Fashion & Flirting, like it says in *That's So Hot!* magazine.

I'm planning to take full advantage of the "Meet-n-Greet" with all those famous authors that the library holds during National Library Week. I had no idea an autographed novel was so valuable. I could collect a half dozen and then sell them on eBay for big bucks.

Then, KA-CHING!! I could buy that cell phone I've been wanting!

Am I NOT brilliant?! ☺!

BTW, I decided to save the $750 prize money for art camp next summer. If I continue to work really hard on my art, I could possibly land a four-year scholarship to a major university. SWEET ☺!!

Brandon stopped by our table to ask if he could interview me about winning the avant-garde art competition, since it was "breaking news."

I thanked him for taking the photographs of my tattoo designs and told him what a great job he had done on them.

But he said it was no biggie, and he planned to use the photos for the article he was writing.

Then MacKenzie came over, acting all friendly, and actually congratulated me. I was so shocked, I almost puked my lunch on her designer shoes!

But I think she really just wanted to flirt with Brandon, because she kept batting her eyes at him all fluttery, like she had accidentally stuck a false eyelash to her eyeball or something.

Yes, MacKenzie is rich, popular, and pretty. But I can't help but wonder if Brandon could actually like a girl who has the IQ of LINT.

In spite of the fact that we had agreed not to do any tattoos until next month, Chloe and Zoey insisted that I do just ONE more for . . .

MYSELF! ...

MY TATTOO WAS AWESOME!

Okay, I admit I was wrong about Grandma being senile. But I was correct about that KA-RAY-ZEE puppet, Miss Penelope.

After lunch was over, Brandon interviewed me for the school newspaper as we walked to my locker.

But I wanted to tell him how much I appreciated him being my friend.

He'd been there with an umbrella during an awful rainstorm. And he had an endless supply of napkins, tissues, and silly burp jokes.

Brandon had seen me covered in various nasty substances, like spaghetti, cherry jubilee, and snot, and STILL wanted to hang out with me.

I had to admit, Brandon was ALMOST as awesome as Chloe and Zoey! That's when I came up with a brilliant idea for how to thank him for everything, including the work he'd done on my art project.

I gave him a very cool TATTOO of that cute but creepy CAMERA BUG I had dreamed about!

For some reason, guys seem to like really weird stuff like that. . . .

ME, GIVING BRANDON A CAMERA BUG TATTOO
WHILE CHLOE AND ZOEY SPY ON US!

"Thanks Nikki! This tattoo ROCKS!" Brandon gushed. "How did you know I like photography?!"

"It was just a lucky guess," I answered.

Then he brushed his bangs out of his eyes with his fingers and smiled at me kind of shylike. "So I . . . um . . . was wondering if you'd like to be lab partners in bio for 'structure of mitochondria'?"

I could NOT believe Brandon asked me that. I just giggled and squealed:

"SQUEEEEEEEEEEEEEEEEEEEEEEEEEEEEEE!!"

I'm sure he thought I was CRAZY. But he just smiled, grabbed his camera, and started snapping photos of me for the newspaper.

Hey, I can only be myself, right?!

I'M SUCH A DORK!!

☺!!

327

ACKNOWLEDGMENTS

I would like to thank everyone who helped to make my dream become a reality: Liesa Abrams, my fantastic editor, for bringing great passion to this project and loving it as much as I did, and designer Lisa Vega, for her keen eye and never-ending patience.

A special thanks to Karin Paprocki, my creative art director. With your exceptional design skills, collaboration, and artistic vision, we've created a fun new cover and classic new artwork that DORK SUPERfans will be sure to enjoy. Thanks for helping me update Nikki's world for a new generation of ADORKABLE fans.

To my league of superheroes at Aladdin/Simon & Schuster, Mara Anastas, Mary Marotta, Jon Anderson, Julie Doebler, Jennifer Romanello, Faye Bi, Carolyn Swerdloff, Tara Grieco, Lucille Rettino, Matt Pantoliano, Michelle Leo, Candace McManus, Anthony Parisi, Sarah McCabe, Emma Sector, Brenna Franzitta, Christina Solazzo, Jeannie Ng, Katherine Devendorf, Bridget Madsen, Rebecca Vitkus, Ellen

Grafton, Matt Jackson, Angela Zurlo, Jenn Rothkin, Christina Pecorale, Gary Urda, and the entire sales force. Thanks for your hard work and commitment.

A special thanks to Torie Doherty-Munro at Writers House; my foreign rights agents Maja Nikolic, Cecilia de la Campa, Angharad Kowal, and James Munro; and Zoé, Marie, and Joy—you are an elite group of crusaders with supernatural abilities.

Nikki Russell, my very talented assistant artist, whose hard work helped to bring this in under deadline.

Doris Edwards, my mom, for being there through thick and thin and always reassuring me that my writing was funny, even when it probably wasn't.

My daughters, Erin and Nikki Russell, for their love and encouragement.

Arianna Robinson, Mikayla Robinson, and Sydney James, my tween-age nieces, for being the sweetest, most fab, and totally brutal critique partners an author could wish for.

Rachel Renée Russell is the #1

New York Times bestselling author of the blockbuster book series Dork Diaries and the bestselling series The Misadventures of Max Crumbly.

There are more than fifty million copies of her books in print worldwide, and they have been translated into forty-two languages.

She enjoys working with her two daughters, Erin and Nikki, who help write and illustrate her books.

Rachel's message is "Always let your inner dork shine through!"

**Read on for a sneak peek
of PARTY TIME!**

FRIDAY, OCTOBER 11

I can't believe this is happening to me!

I'm in the girls' bathroom FREAKING OUT!!

There's NO WAY I'm going to survive middle school.

I've just made a complete FOOL of myself in front of my secret crush. AGAIN ☹!!

And if that wasn't bad enough, I'm still stuck with a locker right next to MacKenzie Hollister's ☹!

Who, BTW, is the most popular girl at Westchester Country Day Middle School and a total SNOB. Calling her a "mean girl" is an understatement.

She's a KILLER SHARK in sparkly nail polish, designer jeans and platform Skechers.

But for some reason, everyone ADORES her.

MacKenzie and I do NOT get along. I'm guessing it's probably due to the fact that she

HATES MY GUTS ☹!!

She is forever gossiping behind my back and saying supermean stuff like that I have no fashion sense whatsoever and that our school mascot, Larry the Lizard, wears cuter clothes than I do.

Which might actually be true. But STILL!

I do NOT appreciate that girl BLABBING about my personal business.

This morning she was even more vicious than usual.

I could NOT believe she actually said that to me!

I mean, how can a COLOR clash with a FLAVOR?!
DUH!! They're, like, two TOTALLY different,
um... THINGS!

That's when I lost it and yelled, "Sorry, MacKenzie!
But I'm REALLY busy right now. Can I IGNORE you
some other time?!"

But I just said it inside my head, so no one else
heard it but me.

And if all of that isn't enough TORTURE, the
annual WCD Halloween dance is in three weeks!

It's the biggest event of the fall, and everyone is
already gossiping about who's going with who.

I'd just totally DIE if my secret crush

 BRANDON

asked me to go!

Yesterday he actually asked ME to be his lab partner for biology class!

I was SO excited, I did my Snoopy "happy dance".

La, La, La!
I'M . . .

La, La, La!
SO . . .

La, La, La!
HAPPY!!

And today I had a sneaking suspicion Brandon was going to "pop the question" about the Halloween dance.

The school day seemed to drag on FOREVER.

By the time I got to biology class, I was a nervous wreck.

Suddenly, a very troubling question popped into my head and I started to panic: what if Brandon only thought of me as a lab partner and nothing more?!

That's when I decided to try to impress him with my charm, wit and intelligence.

I gave him a big smile and went right to work drawing all these teeny-tiny lint-looking thingies I saw under the microscope.

Out of the corner of my eye, I could see Brandon staring at me with this urgent, yet very perplexed, look on his face.

It was obvious he wanted to talk to me about something SUPERserious. . . ☺!

Those thingies in the microscope really WERE just LINT! OMG!! I was SO EMBARRASSED!!

I knew right then and there I had pretty much blown any chance of Brandon asking me to the dance.

But the good news was, I had made a startling scientific discovery about the biogenetics of my intelligence and even reduced it to a working formula.

MY IQ ≤

Then things got even WORSE.

Dirty gym → sock

I was in the girls' bathroom when I overheard MacKenzie bragging to her friends that she was practically almost 99.9% sure she and Brandon were going to the dance together as Edward and Bella from *Twilight*.

I was VERY disappointed, but not the least bit surprised. I mean, WHY would Brandon ask a total DORK like ME when he could go with a CCP (Cute, Cool & Popular) girl like MacKenzie?

And get this! As they were leaving, MacKenzie giggled and said she was buying a new lip gloss JUST for Brandon. I knew what THAT meant.

I was SO frustrated and angry at myself.

I waited until the bathroom was empty, and then I had a really good SCREAM.

Which, for some strange reason, always makes me feel a lot better ☺.

Middle school can be very TRAUMATIZING, that's for sure!!

But the most important thing to remember is this: always remain CALM and try to handle your personal problems in a PRIVATE and MATURE manner.

ME, HAVING A PRIVATE SCREAM-FEST!